Carl Weber's:

Five Families of New York

Part 2: Harlem

Carl Weber's:

Five Families of New York

Part 2: Harlem

C. N. Phillips

www.urbanbooks.net

Urban Books, LLC
300 Farmingdale Road, NY-Route 109
Farmingdale, NY 11735

Carl Weber's: Five Families of New York Part 2: Harlem
Copyright © 2021 C. N. Phillips

ISBN 13: 978-1-64556-283-2
ISBN 10: 1-64556-283-2

First Mass Market Printing February 2022
First Trade Paperback Printing August 2021
Printed in the United States of America

10 9 8 7 6 5 4 3 2 1

*This is a work of fiction. Any references or similarities
to actual events, real people, living or dead, or to real
locales are intended to give the novel a sense of reality.
Any similarity in other names, characters, places, and
incidents is entirely coincidental.*

Distributed by Kensington Publishing Corp.
Submit Orders to:
Customer Service
400 Hahn Road
Westminster, MD 21157-4627
Phone: 1-800-733-3000
Fax: 1-800-659-2436

Prologue

Numb. That was how Boogie's body felt after all his emotions hit at once. He didn't know if he had been driving too fast or too slow on the highway. All he knew was somehow he made it home. Once there, he had half a mind to go back to the auto shop and murder Caesar the same way he'd done Julius. The same way he'd done Barry. Boogie didn't know why he had left him with breath still in him. He'd just been so shocked. He couldn't believe that it had been Caesar all along.

He didn't know how long he was just sitting in his car, but eventually Boogie found himself inside his condo with a suitcase in his hands. He began packing it without pausing to take a break. The anger and sorrow inside of him were so powerful that he needed to get away for a while before he did something foolish. He knew he would be letting his father down by running away, but he didn't want any of it anymore. The empire, the responsibility. He'd just taken his seat at the table, but now he felt like saying to hell with it all. If he had let a snake like Caesar close to him without knowing he was slimy, then obviously he wasn't ready to be a leader.

He had just zipped his suitcase when he heard the front door to his condo open and slam shut. He quickly pulled his pistol out and pointed it at his bedroom doorway as he listened to the footsteps walking down the hallway. He just knew Caesar was coming to finish the job, so when the person appeared in the doorway, he had his finger positioned on the trigger.

"You're going to shoot your own mother?" Dina asked, raising a brow at the pistol pointed at her.

"Mama, what are you doin' here?" Boogie asked, putting the gun away. He took in her appearance. She looked tired and was dressed in a black jogging suit. "You can't just be showin' up places without callin'. Dressed like the cat burglar at that."

"I did call. About five times. When you didn't answer, something told me to come check on my baby boy," she said and looked at the packed suitcase on the bed. "Going somewhere?"

"Yeah, far away from here."

"What?" she asked, concerned. "Boogie, baby, talk to me. Don't leave."

"I got to, Ma."

"You sound silly. No you do—"

"Yes, I do!" Boogie barked at her. "I don't want shit to do with none of this anymore. Understand?"

"None of what, Boogie? Talk to me."

He didn't want to talk, though. He wanted to shout and keep on shouting until he had no voice left. Desolate, Boogie slightly raised his arms at his side and let them fall. He sat down on the bed and shook his head.

"You were right," he said and balled his fists. "Mama, you were right about Caesar. He was behind everything. He killed my pops."

"What?" Dina asked with a look of shock on her face. "Caesar killed your father?"

Boogie nodded, and her hand went to her chest. She went and sat next to him on the bed, taking his hand in hers. He barely felt her sympathetic squeeze. All the time he'd spent with Caesar flashed in his head. He'd rode with him, ate with him, and laughed with him. It must have all been sick fun to take in the son of the man you murdered. Caesar had put on a good face, so good that before, Boogie would have argued his innocence. Now he would never.

"I knew it. I told you that motherfucka wasn't no good. He was always jealous of Barry. And when your father didn't do what Caesar wanted, he'd signed his own death wish."

"That's not all, Mama," Boogie said and looked in her eyes. "Tonight, at Big Wheels, I walked in on Julius dead and Caesar behind the gun. He killed Unc too."

"And you didn't kill him?" Dina asked. Her question caught him off guard. "The man who murdered your father and your uncle was in front of you, and you didn't kill him?"

"I–I couldn't. I was stuck, and I guess I just couldn't believe what I was seeing. I never wanted to believe that he's a monster."

"Well, he is. Or should I say was."

"Was?" Boogie asked, and she nodded.

"They found him and Bosco dead tonight. They announced it on the news on my way over here. I'm thinking what might have happened is that Caesar killed Bosco, and his people came after him."

"But why would Caesar kill Bosco?"

"Because he was a selfish bastard!"

"Even still, it doesn't make sense."

"But doesn't it? If you knock all the unwanted chess pieces off the board, all that's left is the king."

"Now the chess board is all fucked up. There's no balance."

"There will be if you stay put," Dina said, giving her son a knowing look. *"New York needs a new king. It needs someone who doesn't need a pact to tell him what to do. It needs you, Boogie. And you'll have something none of the other heads have."*

"What's that?"

"Three territories."

"But I don't have three territories."

"You will," Dina said, patting his shoulder. *"With both Caesar and Bosco gone, their empires will be scrambling to function. And if chaos breaks out in Manhattan, it will spread everywhere. Including Brooklyn."*

"How do you know so much about the game?" Boogie asked her, and she turned her lip up at him.

"When your father met me, I wasn't some wholesome schoolgirl. I was selling coke out of a one-bedroom apartment with a gun on my hip with three other girls. I know the game because I was in the game. I gave your father the start-up money for his first business, and he made me his wife."

"I never knew that." Boogie gave her a look of wonder.

"Well, now you do, and son, you aren't going anywhere. Plans . . . hm. They switch up every day," she said and cleared her throat. *"Now, I didn't want you anywhere around any of this. I wanted more for you. I wanted you to be the chef that you always wanted to be, but now, things are different. When a leprechaun leaves you his pot of gold, you take it. Fuck the five families, because the families fucked us. Do you hear me?"*

"Yeah, I hear you."

"So, what are you going to do about it?"

"Take over New York."

Chapter 1

The night was still young, but the colorful strobe lights in the Sugar Trap bounced off many paying patrons. One of the patrons was paying close attention to a thick redbone with knee-length braids. He sat at the stage, watching her twirl around the pole and twerking her round bottom just for him—or that's what it seemed like. Suddenly, she dropped into a split and bounced up and down a few times. After she did that a few more times, he waved her over. She grinned at him as she seductively crawled to him, then she sat at the edge of the stage with her legs open, giving him a perfect view of the plumpness in her green G-string.

"Scotty, this is the third night this week I've seen you here. You came to give me more of your money?"

"Thunder, you know you're my favorite girl in the whole world. I don't know why you keep playin' with me."

Thunder gave a forced giggle, the way she did with all of her customers. Scotty was a handsome man in his mid-twenties, who came in the club thirsty for her whenever he could. Although Scotty didn't come in and spend big cash on her, he still spent a small bag, and she needed to pay her rent and car note, which were late since she just *had* to have those three YSL bags. She was going to work him for all that he'd come there with by any means necessary.

Scotty dressed like he was the big boss in charge, but he wasn't. He was a runner for a few of Caesar's underbosses. Still, he made his paper, and she knew he had at least five thousand on him right then and there. She eyeballed the three empty glasses on the table next to him and saw that he was working on his fourth drink. She licked her lips seductively and stared into his tipsy eyes.

"Boy, ain't nobody playing with you. You playing with me."

"How am I doin' that?"

"Because you're sitting in front of me looking like a boss, all dripped in Gucci and shit, but you only done threw about five hundred at your so-called favorite girl. What I'ma do with that?" Thunder pouted.

"I would give a lot more if I could touch you," he said, biting his lip.

"Then come on so I can give you a private dance." She nodded her head toward the area with the private rooms.

"Nah," Scotty said. "I mean, I wanna *touch* you. Not just a dance."

His eyes lowered to her plump pussy and then back up to her face. He didn't even need to do all of that for Thunder to understand what he was talking about. She caught his drift. She smacked her lips at him.

"Scotty, you know how Diana feels about fucking in her club," Thunder said, referring to the owner of the Sugar Trap. "She'll kill us both if she catches us."

"I got two bands on top of that five hundred if you're willin' to take that risk. Girl, I know I am. You know how bad I been wantin' you. Come on."

She weighed her options. Diana wasn't someone to mess with, but still, all Thunder could think about was the money. She knew he was good for it. And, after all, her bills weren't going to pay themselves. She looked at his lustful face and could tell by how drunk he was that he might not even last three minutes inside of her waterfall. It was a win-win for her.

Thunder got down from the stage, grabbing her money bag and his hand. She took Scotty to a stairway that was guarded by two big-body Dominican bouncers.

"Dru, we're headed up to the Passion Room," she said to one of them.

He didn't say anything back to her. Instead, he looked Scotty over before stepping out of the way.

Thunder's six-inch stilettos stabbed the red carpet as she led Scotty up the rounded staircase and down a hallway. Inside the Passion Room, she shut the door behind her. Girls weren't allowed to lock the door, but that was all right. She didn't plan to be there long.

The blue light gave the room a sultry feel, and Thunder pushed Scotty through a curtain to the back of the room, where the big furry white couch was. She turned on some sexy R&B to get the mood right.

"I'm going to need at least half up front before any-thing goes down," she told him, removing her green top.

The moment he saw the chocolate nipples on her perky breasts, Scotty got to digging in his pockets. He pulled out a fold of hundreds and hurried to count ten. She took them and recounted them just to make sure it was all there. Stuffing the cash into her money bag and setting it to the side, she glanced at the clock. All private dances in the Passion Room were twenty minutes. Anything over and the bouncer would come to check on things. The clock was ticking, and Thunder wanted her other thousand, so she got straight to work. She knew Scotty was on the same page, because when she looked back at him, his dick was out, and he was rolling a condom down on it. He was a nice size, and Thunder was almost sad that she was going to have to rush his nut out.

She moved close to him before turning around so that her butt was in his face, and then she bent over. He moved the G-string to the side and plunged in headfirst. The way he licked her ass crack up and slurped on her sweet pussy let her know that he really had been wanting her for a while. Her hands were on her knees, and she clapped her butt cheeks on his face as he devoured her. His tongue swiveled around her clit before he pulled it back and plunged it in and out of her opening. When she felt his finger apply pressure to her butthole, she pushed down on her stomach the way a person would when they had to fart, to open her hole. Anal was one of her favorites, and she bit her lip when he forced his finger inside of her. He had her feeling so good that she almost wanted him to keep pleasing her just like that until she came, but she didn't have time for that. She twerked on his tongue a few more times before pulling away and forcing his finger out of her butt.

Looking back at him, she slowly lowered her wet cat down on his rock-hard manhood. He slid inside of her easily, and one of his eyes twitched from that first wave of pleasure. She then commenced to bouncing up and down mercilessly on him. He reached his arms around and fondled her breasts and nipples.

"Damn, Thunder," he moaned behind her. "I knew this pussy was gon' be fire."

His dick felt good inside of her too, but she was trying hard not to focus on that. She spun around to face him with her heels on the couch. She placed her hands on his shoulders to balance herself when he slid inside of her again.

Scotty spread her ass cheeks apart as he drilled into her, moaning and making all kinds of faces. Thunder wanted to laugh so hard at the fact that the pussy was driving him so crazy, but she didn't. He nibbled on her nipples, leaving spit trails when he went from one to the other as she rode him harder and faster.

"Oh, fuck!" He moaned loudly, and Thunder felt his nails dig into her skin.

Scotty clenched his eyes shut, and his body jerked a few times as he shot his cum into the condom with his dick still inside of her. Thunder felt it throbbing and waited for it to stop before she got off of him. He tried to catch his breath while she wiped herself with one of the wet wipes in the Passion Room and adjusted her G-string.

After grabbing her top off the ground, she turned back to him. He threw the condom in the trash and was pulling up his pants. Thunder made a mental note to grab the used condom and dispose of it somewhere else so no one would know what she had done.

"I'll take the rest of my money now," she said, and Scotty looked at her like she was crazy before giving a small laugh.

"You gon' take that fifteen hundred and be happy," he told her.

She didn't like the way his tone had changed or what he had said to her. It was unbelievable. She looked at him as if he had feces all over his face.

"Uh, nah, nigga. You said you were going to pay me two bands, and I want the other half of that. Right now and pronto."

"Bitch, you crazy," he said, standing to his feet. "I got what I wanted. Now I'm about to bounce."

Thunder was just about to pull out her shank and make the childish smile he wore permanent, when suddenly the music stopped. Replacing it was the sound of a lighter and a slow drawl of what smelled like the best weed in New York. There was a silhouette on the other side of the curtain, and Thunder's heart stopped before the person moved it out of the way—mainly because there was only one person in the club who was allowed to smoke weed in the building.

"D–Diana," Thunder stuttered when she finally stepped through the curtain.

Diana was a five-foot-five Dominican woman who didn't look to be a day over forty, although she was in her sixties. She was beautiful——no, stunning—but her beauty was only cushion for her bite. She stood in front of them wearing a red pantsuit that clung to her slender and fit figure, with her long black hair in one French braid going down her back.

Her dark brown eyes pierced Thunder's. She didn't have to say what she was thinking, nor did her anger have to show on her face. Thunder knew the rules of the Sugar Trap, and the fact that she had gone against them showed how little respect she had for the establishment. Diana didn't know if she was angrier at Thunder or Scotty for refusing to give what was promised. Either way, they both would pay.

"Do you know the price of disobeying me?" she asked in a smooth, mature tone while looking at Thunder.

"N–no," Thunder stammered.

"Your life."

Faster than either of them could react, Diana pulled a small .22 from the waist of her pants and shot her neatly in the center of her forehead. She dropped like a sack of potatoes. Diana shook her head at her dead body.

"Tsk tsk. She was one of my best girls," she said and picked up Thunder's sack of money before turning to Scotty. "And you? You promised her two thousand dollars to disrespect me?"

"D–Diana, wait," Scotty said, looking at the gun in her hand.

"And now you're telling me what to do," she scoffed. "I need to make a mental note to tell Caesar that his pawns are getting beside themselves. I might not be able to kill you, but I can cause you a great deal of pain. Or . . ."

"Or what? I'll do anything."

"You're in debt to me until you die. Two thousand a week, every week. The only time I want to see you in my establishment from here on out is when you are bringing me my money. Do you understand me?"

"Y–yes."

"Now get the fuck out."

He ran past her to the door. When she heard it shut and she was alone with Thunder's body, she found herself staring at the blood spilling from her head. Normally, Diana wouldn't touch a hair on her girls' heads, but once you broke the rules, you were no longer one of her girls. She pulled out her cell phone and called down to Dru.

"Everything good? I saw Scotty run out of here like he had fire on his ass."

"Things will be better if you send a mop up here and hire the best girl from tonight's Amateur Night. Thunder quit."

"Will do," was all Dru said before Diana disconnected the call.

She exited the Passion Room and put the closed sign on the door, knowing that Dru was about to send a cleaner team. She sighed as she walked down the curved staircase, through the large crowd of people on the main floor, and to a hallway in the back of the building that led to her spacious office.

She'd been in the middle of watching a rerun episode *of Jerry Springer*, and she wanted to see what the girl would do when she found out her man had slept with her cousin. She never made it that far, though. Her phone buzzed in her pocket, and upon seeing Marco's name pop up, she answered on the second ring.

"Hello?"

"Diana? Where are you?" Marco asked in a rushed tone.

"I'm at the club. Is everything all right?" Diana asked, stopping in her tracks.

"No, everything isn't," he said, and from the panic in his voice, she knew something terrible had to have happened. Marco never panicked.

"What happened?"

"It's Caesar," he said. "He's—"

"Dead?" Diana asked and dreaded the answer to come.

"Alive," Marco finished. "But barely. He was shot. Please come. We need your help. I'm at the Big House."

"Okay. I'm on my way."

Chapter 2

Diana drove down a barely lit winding road until she reached the gates of a large estate. Many of the lights inside were on, and in the distance, she saw cars parked on the roundabout by the front walkway. She recognized the man at the front gates as the same man who had been guarding them for years. Malcom was in his mid-thirties and had been working for Caesar since he was a teenage boy. He was what most would call all right looking, but what he lacked in looks, he made up for in muscle. A while back, he got bumped up with some drugs on him, but he never said a word. He laid down for five years, and when he got out, Caesar rewarded him by taking him off the streets completely.

Malcom had always been a man with keen eyes and even sharper shooting. Not only that, but he had proven to be worthy of being a part of The Trusted, the ones the five families regarded above all else because their loyalty was unwavering. And as part of The Trusted, Malcom was put in charge of guarding the one place only a handful of people even knew existed—the estate of the five families, aka the Big House. It was built and paid for by all of them and was supposed to be a fortress that offered sanctuary if anything were to ever happen to them. Up until then, it had only been used for a few meetings, never for its intended purpose. But now, it served as the perfect place to hide Caesar.

"Everyone else is here," Malcom told her as he pressed a button to open the gates.

"Thank you, Malcom," she said and pulled her sapphire green Jaguar through.

Diana couldn't park fast enough behind Marco's blue Tesla. She hopped out of the car and moved as fast as her legs would take her. Bursting through the tall double doors of the house, she raced up the curved staircase and to the second level of the four-story home.

"Marco! Li!" She called out multiple times as she opened doors to every room she passed.

"Down here. In the master," Marco called from the very last room in the hallway.

Diana half walked and half jogged to the master bedroom. It was a large room, and lying lifeless on the bed inside it was Caesar. She forced herself to keep breathing because she had never seen him in such a state. Time seemed to pause for a beat as she just stared, but movement in the corner of her eye reminded her that she wasn't alone.

Li sat in a chair on one side of the bed, while Marco stood at the foot of it. Their hurt expressions explained how she felt inside. For almost forty years, the five of them had been like family. They would never admit it because they ran their own separate factions, but at the end of the day, it always came back to them. Now, with Barry dead and Caesar fighting for his life, the world around them just didn't feel right.

There was a young blonde nurse in the room, who was currently adjusting Caesar's pillows, and Diana cleared her throat to get her attention.

"Can we have a moment please?"

"Of course," the young woman said with a pleasant tone then left the room.

Diana closed the door behind her and went to Caesar's side. She didn't know why she thought his eyes would open the harder she looked at his eyelids. When they didn't, she felt a lump form in her throat.

"Who did this to him?" Diana demanded to know, and Li and Marco looked at each other. "Don't do that. Tell me what you know."

"We can't be for sure, but word is Caesar made a move on the Italians, and now Bosco is dead," Marco told her.

"What? Why would he do that?" Diana asked.

"I think we can all agree that he's been a little aloof since Barry died," Marco said.

"Yeah, but that still doesn't explain why he would do something like kill Bosco."

"We don't know, but if Caesar did something that fucking crazy, we know there had to be a reason. The man doesn't even take a piss unless he absolutely has to."

"True, but him not saying anything to us doesn't sound like him at all."

"That's what we were sitting here trying to figure out," Li said. "None of us has ever made a move like that without consulting with the families."

"Hmm." Diana wracked her mind. "So, what you're telling me is that you think the Italians retaliated against him?"

"I can't say for sure, but it would make sense."

"No, that's the thing. None of this makes sense at all." Diana clenched her jaw. Caesar had taught her a long time ago that things were never as easy as they seemed to be. "First Barry gets killed, then some fucking random drug dealers start making moves around Brooklyn, and now Bosco is dead. All this shit ties into each other. It can't be a coincidence."

"But how?" Li asked.

"That's what we need to figure out. Has anybody actually spoken to Boogie? Set up a meeting as soon as possible. Somebody is out there taking shots at us one by one, and we will be stronger together than separate."

"You haven't heard?" Li asked.

"If you're talking about the message Boogie sent saying he wants out, yes, I got that. But I don't care what he said. We all owe it to Caesar to get to the bottom of this. Especially me."

Diana turned her eyes back to Caesar and almost couldn't take seeing him with so much equipment attached to his body. It reminded her that he was just a man. Even he wasn't untouchable. Her mind flashed her back to 1978, when she had first met him, reminding her why it was so important to her to find out who had done that to him.

"Papá, all my girls are out shopping. And I'm the only one not there!" A seventeen-year-old Diana pouted.

She leaned her head into the leather headrest of the Cadillac and looked out the window. Although Diana loved spending time with her old father, Domino, she would much rather be trying on cute clothes with her friends. Lately, ever since she had turned seventeen, her dad had been making her ride with him on his runs. Domino, born Dominic Reyes, was what some would call a pimp, but Diana knew that he was much more than that. Her father was a businessman in and out. The many women who worked for him understood that their most prized possession was between their legs. There was a reason why the vagina was shaped like a wallet, and they knew it. However, selling sex for a living was a dangerous game, especially for a young woman in the streets of New York, which was why they always had security not too far from them. If a John got out of line or tried to skip out on payment, he would quickly get put back into his place. Domino had all of Harlem on lock, but his girls made their way around a little of everywhere.

Diana wasn't naïve. She knew the reason her father allowed her to know even half of what he did was because he was grooming her. She was very mature for her young age and could count money in her sleep. Being his only child, she could see why he would want to pass something on to her, and although she still wanted to have fun doing the normal things that girls her age did, she couldn't lie. She liked the power she had just from being Dominic Reyes' daughter.

She especially liked the lifestyle it came with. At that moment, she had a ten-thousand-dollar diamond choker casually around her neck. On her feet were a pair of Gucci sandals on her freshly pedicured toes. The things that were so normal to her, others would sell their souls *to have. And all of it came courtesy of being a Reyes. Her father wasn't just a pimp; he was one of the most feared men in Harlem and one of the most feared in New York.*

"I just have to make one stop, and then I will take you to wherever you want to go. Okay, Princess?"

"All right." Diana pouted. "Where are we going anyways?"

"I have to grab a suitcase in Manhattan," he said. She knew that meant he was going to pick up a payment.

"From who?"

"Paul."

"Hm," was all she said, but Domino recognized her unapproving tone.

"What's that for?"

"I don't know, Papá, I just don't like him much."

"Paul?" Domino chuckled. "What don't you like about him?"

Paul was a businessman who often threw a lot of parties that he liked filled with whores. It was no secret that the allure of beautiful women softened men up to spend big money. Domino was always Paul's go-to man when it came to getting clean girls. The truth was that Diana knew why she didn't like Paul, but she doubted that it would make a difference in his business dealings with her father.

Diana had been to one of the houses where Domino kept his girls. Although Domino didn't like for her to go there, she would go anyway. They were always so nice to her, being as she was the boss's daughter, but after one of Paul's events, they were different. They didn't speak to her, nor would they look in her eyes. When she asked the head girl, Monet, what was wrong, she would always say, "Paul's boys are wild." And that was it. Monet never went into detail, but whatever it meant, it wasn't good.

"Has Monet ever told you about how Paul's men treat them?"

"She may have said they were a little rough, but I talked to Paul about that."

"That's all?" Diana asked.

"He knows what will happen to him if something happens to one of mine. Also, my girls know what they signed up for when they chose their lifestyle. Some men like . . . different things. And they deliver."

"I still don't like him." Diana shrugged. "Even whores deserve to be treated with respect. They're there to make you feel good, so you'd have to be a scumbag to be bad to her."

Domino glanced humorously at his daughter's defiant face. She was a feisty thing, just like her mother had been. Not only that, but she had a certain compassion about her that he admired. It was something that could be considered a weakness in the field; however, Domino knew a day would come when Diana would lose her compassion. She would become coldhearted just like the rest of them. It was inevitable. The things she would see and go up against would eventually turn her heart merciless, but still, he wanted her to hold onto the goodness in her heart for as long as she could.

"We're here," Domino announced after driving a little longer.

Diana, who had gone back to leaning her head into her headrest, looked out the window to see where they were.

Usually, her father met Domino somewhere fancy, but that day, they were parked outside of a regular house that she had never been to before. There were some younger men sitting on the stoop, while others stood around the house, holding beers in their hands. They weren't alone. Outside with them, looking slightly uncomfortable, were a few of Domino's girls. It was a hot summer day, so they were standing there in short shorts and crop tops. One thing about Domino was he only had beautiful and shapely women working for him.

She recognized one of them as Vy, a new girl Domino had recently acquired. Although she was out there with some vets, Diana could sense that she was tense.

"I'll be right back, sweetheart," Domino said before stepping out of the car.

Diana barely nodded her response. She was too busy watching the man who was standing next to Vy. At a glance, it seemed as if he were holding her elbow gently, but Diana could see Vy secretly trying to tug away. It wasn't until everyone saw Domino walking up that he let her go. They all grew quiet and still. Even the brown pit bull stopped barking and sat down as Domino approached.

"Hi, Daddy!" a young woman they called Cupcake said when he walked past her.

"Papi!" another named Luna gushed. "We did not expect you for another few hours. The party is still going on inside. But we can hurr—"

"I'm not here to stop the party. I'm here to collect, so you girls better make every penny Paul is spending worth it. Understand?" Domino asked and surveyed the women outside.

"Of course, Daddy!" They all said in unison, except one.

Domino didn't catch it, but Diana did. Vy hadn't opened her mouth once, which was strange. When Domino recruited her, Diana had been there. Vy was a dancer that Domino had pulled down from the pole with the promise of even more money. She'd only been working for him for two months, but in that month, she had been nice and quirky. She turned her tricks and made her dues with no problem. From what Diana had seen, the girl knew how to talk the talk, so her behavior in that moment wasn't sitting right with Diana.

When Domino disappeared inside the house, the people outside went back to drinking and laughing; however, the smile on Cupcake's face dropped. She grabbed Vy and pulled her over to the side. Diana couldn't make out what Cupcake was saying to Vy, but she could tell by the shaken look on Vy's face that it wasn't nice.

After a few moments, Vy went back over to the man she had been talking to before. Gone was the look of disdain, only to be replaced with a flirty smile and batting eyes. Diana was about to get out of the car to make sure that everything was all right when a set of knuckles appeared, knocking on her window.

"You a new girl or somethin'?" The voice belonged to one of the men she'd seen sitting on the stoop. *"Get on out this car and come have some fun. We won't bite unless you want us to."*

He gave a small laugh that made Diana's stomach turn. She had been so engrossed in Cupcake and Vy that she hadn't even seen the man walk up on the car. She had half a mind to pretend like she didn't see or hear him, but she also wanted to set him straight. She rolled her *window down and looked him slowly from his head to the sneakers on his feet.*

"Do I look like one of those girls?" she said, motioning to the designer fashions that draped her body. "Now, get away from my father's car."

"Oh, shit." A realization washed over his face as he made the connection. "My bad, beautiful. You're Domino's daughter."

"I thought we just made that clear." She rolled her eyes.

"Yeah, we did," he said and continued to stare at her. "I'm Robert. What's your name?"

"Diana."

"Diana, hm. I like that. How old are you, Miss Diana?"

"Almost eighteen."

"So, seventeen," Robert stated.

"Yeah, so?" Diana made a face. "How old are you?"

"Twenty-one," he answered with a smug smile. "Has anybody ever told you how pretty you are, Diana?"

"Yeah, my father does every day. My father also wouldn't like it if he knew that a grown-ass man was at his car, flirting with his underage daughter."

"I feel you," Robert said and put his hands up. "I'm glad you're not a whore, because I don't pay for pussy."

"Then what are you doing here?"

"Hey, this is on somebody else's dime." Robert shrugged. "Anyways, since you aren't one of them, I was going to see if you wanted to come through later. But since I don't have any business talking to you, never mind."

"I wouldn't have come through anyway. You aren't my type."

"You don't even know me to know if I'm your type or not. You aren't the only one up under somebody with a name."

"Yeah, whatever," Diana said in a dismissive tone. She pulled the sun visor down and checked her lip gloss. *"I hope you have fun later. I just want my papá to hurry up because I have some shopping to do at The Strip."*

On her last word, she saw Domino leaving the house, holding a briefcase. His eyes turned to daggers when he saw Robert standing next to his car. He held his cold stare even when Robert backed away with an apprehensive expression. Even Diana sat up slightly in her seat just in case she had to hop out and stop her father from killing somebody. When Domino was only a few feet away from Robert, he looked from Diana to Robert.

"Don't you ever speak to my daughter again. Understand me?"

"Y–yes, sir."

And surprisingly, that was it. Diana let out the breath she had been holding and rolled her window back up. Domino got in the car and fixed the collar on his Versace shirt before starting the car and pulling off.

"What were you doing talking to that trash?"

"I'm sorry, Papá. It won't happen again."

"You're right it won't. I will have to send a message to Caesar and let him know that you are off limits to everybody in his camp."

"That was one of Caesar's hands?"

"Yes."

"Well, why was he at one of Paul's parties?"

"Paul knows many people." Domino shrugged. *"As long as he pays me my money, and as long as Caesar understands his boundaries, there will be no problem."*

"Okay," Diana said.

After a few minutes passed, she looked at her father with hopeful eyes. "So, now that that's done, can I go shopping? If we hurry, we can catch up with Marie and MiKayla!"

A while later, Domino dropped his daughter outside of a line of boutiques in Manhattan after they saw MiKayla's car parked not too far away. Diana was just happy that her girls were still there. She hoped that Marie hadn't gotten the white-and-blue plaid dress that they'd both seen the last time they were there. Diana had the cutest shoes to go with it, and Marie knew that. Marie also knew that if she got it, then Diana wouldn't want the outfit anymore.

Before she got out of the car, she grabbed her purse and gave her father a kiss on the cheek. "Bye, Papá. I will have MiKayla bring me home."

"No. Blakey will come scoop you in an hour. The last time you caught a ride with MiKayla, you were two hours late coming home."

"Ugh, Papá," she whined, *but when Domino raised one brow, she knew there was no point. "Fine. There's MiKayla! I'll see you later."*

She decided it would be best to hurry out of the car before he changed his mind about letting her go period. She'd spotted her friends leaving one of the stores with chocolate shakes in their hands. They smiled big when they saw Diana coming their way.

"What? Daddy let you come out to play?" Marie teased when she reached them.

"Don't say it like he keeps me locked up," Diana said, *making a face. "And please tell me you didn't hit all the good shops in The Strip without me!"*

The Strip was a newer shopping experience in Manhattan and had quickly turned into the hip place to go to get the latest trends. There weren't any designer stores, just small boutiques and eateries, which was always refreshing, given the high-end lives that they were used to. Marie's father was an architect, and MiKayla's father was a lawyer, so they all lived a high-end lifestyle, especially as girls of color. Although all three girls had a boatload of designers in their closets, they enjoyed shopping like regular girls sometimes.

"No, we didn't. You came just in time, too. We were about to go into Amanda's," MiKayla said and linked arms with the other two.

Amanda's was the shop where they'd seen the cute plaid outfit that Diana just had to have. She glanced over at Marie, who was giving her a knowing look.

"You can get the outfit. I don't even want it anymore. I want to find a cute crop top to go with these jeans I just got over at Emery's," she said and held up a shopping bag.

"Good, 'cause girl, I was prepared to fight to the death!"

"I knew you were. Especially since I knew that you already bought those cute platforms to wear with it."

"Mm-hmm. I'm going to be too fine. Okay?"

"If your dad even lets you wear it out of the house!" MiKayla joked.

"My papá wouldn't care about me wearing that. It's not even very revealing."

"Yeah, I'm sure he doesn't care what you wear, as long as you don't look nothing like those women he's always with. You know people say he's a pimp, right? Because he always has different women with him. Hell, sometimes three at a time."

"My papá is a single man and can do whatever he wants." Diana shrugged. *"And he's not a pimp. He's a businessman."*

"A businessman of what?" Marie pried.

"Sales. I've told you that before."

"Well, he must sell something pretty valuable because the house you live in is even bigger than mine! And both my parents are lawyers," Mikayla retorted.

"The difference between us is that I don't care what your parents do for a living. So you can stop asking so many questions about mine," Diana told them.

She looked back to see if her father's car was still there. She just knew it was, because he was just *that* dad. But, surprisingly, he was gone. She exhaled in relief and smiled at the thought of not being on his radar, even if it was just for an hour.

It wasn't always like that. He used to make one of his men go with her everywhere until she made the biggest fuss about it. Now, he still made someone come with her most places, but sometimes he would let her be a regular teen—as long as she carried a .22 in her purse.

They were almost to Amanda's when they heard a lot of commotion in the street behind them. Diana ignored it because all she was focused on was the outfit on the mannequin standing in the window. However, beside her, Mikayla turned her head to see what was going on, and her eyes grew wide.

"Diana!" she shouted and gripped her friend's arm tighter.

Diana turned her head to see what the fuss was about only to see men with masks over their faces running up on them. The girls tried to run, but it was too late—well, for Diana, anyway. The men seemed to have no interest in the other girls. They simply pushed them out of the way and snatched Diana up in their arms. She screamed, but nobody came to help her. They ran with a flailing Diana and threw her in the back of a van.

"No!" she screamed and tried to jump out, but a powerful blow to the head stopped that attempt.

She fell back with a painful grunt. Just before everything around her faded away, she saw the men slam the back of the van door shut after they hopped in with her. The tires of the vehicle screeching was the last sound she heard before the world went blank.

Chapter 3

A sharp sting on the side of Diana's face jarred her awake. She could barely keep her eyes open, and her head hung with her chin to her chest. She moaned softly at the throbbing pain in her temple, and all she wanted to do was go back to sleep. Her eyes closed again, but only briefly. A rough hand found its way to her face and slapped her quickly twice.

"Aht aht. Wakey wakey, Sleeping Beauty," a man's voice sounded.

She moaned again and went to put her hand to her forehead but found that she couldn't. There was something stopping her from raising either arm, and through blurred vision, she saw that she was bound to a chair. Alarmed, she tried to pull herself free, but it was no use.

"You aren't going anywhere anytime soon," the man said.

That voice. She recognized it. Her head felt so heavy, but she lifted it to focus on his face. As his features became clearer, her recent memories of being snatched away from her friends came back to her. She'd been kidnapped, and when she saw by who, she was confused.

"Robert?" she asked. "What the fuck are you doing?"

"A little bit of this, a little bit of that," Robert shrugged with a smirk.

They were in the very dimly lit living room area of a small house with older furnishings. Looking around, Diana saw that they weren't alone. She recognized another face from the house she'd gone to with her father earlier that day, as well as a few others. The way they were all staring at her made her skin crawl.

"If my father finds out, he's going to murder all of you."

"See, that's where you have it wrong. I actually am counting on him finding out, but if he doesn't do what we want, it's going to be his sweet princess that ends up dead," Robert said and knelt down in front of her. "How much do you think he'd pay to have you back? I'm thinking half a mil—hell, maybe a mil. We won't know until we ask."

Diana spat in his face, causing him to clench his eyes shut. In a fit of anger, Robert backhanded her and then grabbed her by the back of her hair. She breathed rigidly as she tried to stomach the pain from the blow. Her teeth bared as she glared up at him.

"Do you think you and your little boy scouts are going to be able to stop Domino Reyes' wrath?" Diana asked, ignoring the feeling of her hair follicles ripping from her scalp.

"Didn't I tell you earlier that you weren't the only one connected to somebody powerful? Your father isn't the only one who makes niggas shake in their boots."

"Oh, yeah? I'd like to know one man who can go toe to toe with my papá."

Robert looked at her with a sinister smile before saying a name that made Diana's heart drop to her stomach.

"Caesar."

"*Caesar?*" *she asked almost in a whisper.* "*Caesar ordered this hit on my papá?*"

"*Let's just say muthafuckas are tired of sharing turf.*"

Diana couldn't believe it. She knew all about Caesar. She knew he was ruthless and a force to be reckoned with. He was only about eighteen years old, but when his father had died, he took on the role as New York's drug kingpin. What she didn't know was that he had any kind of beef with her father. For the most part, her father and the other men who ran New York played by the same rules. There was a time recently where there was much feuding going on all around, but it had seemed to slow down.

"*Snatching you up was just the first move of many to come,*" *Robert said.*

Although he still had her hair in an airtight grip, Diana saw the men around him glance quickly at him. She didn't know what those looks were about. She couldn't read them. Before she had time to say anything else, the front door to the house opened and another man entered. Diana recognized him as the man that was giving one of the girls a hard time at the party. The alarmed feeling she had came back when she noticed he wasn't alone. In his arms, barely able to walk, was Vy.

"*What's going on, Tracy? Why you got this bitch with you?*" *Robert asked, letting go of Diana's hair.*

"*This hoe ain't wanna give me no pussy back at Paul's party,*" *Tracy answered, looking down at Vy.* "*And shit, I thought that was what Caesar had the motherfucka set the shit up for. We ran up two hundred thousand in the streets this week for that nigga. The least I can get is some pussy from a whore!*"

"Vy," Diana said, trying to get her attention, but whenever Vy's eyes found Diana's through her barely open eyelids, they rolled in the back of her head. She was high out of her mind.

"What did you do to her?" Diana asked.

Whatever Vy had been slipped had her in bad shape. She couldn't stand on her own and was leaning onto Tracy for support. Tracy had been so focused on Vy that he barely noticed the girl tied to a chair in the middle of the living room. He looked at her and then he looked at Robert.

"What the fuck you got going on here? Is this who I think it is?"

"Yeah, nigga," Robert boasted. "Snatched her ass up at The Strip earlier today. She's gon' get up them big coins."

"Damn, nigga, you're a bold one. What you gon' do if—"

"That ain't gon' happen." Robert quickly cut in and glanced at Diana. "I got it all under control. Plus, by the time her daddy pays up the money, she'll be dead already. No trace."

"Yeah, a'ight," Tracy said and shook his head dismissively. "You handle your business and I'ma go handle mine."

He tried to take Vy by the hand, but she snatched away. He tried again, and she did the same thing. The men sitting and standing around laughed.

"Yo, Tracy, even high off that shit she don't wanna fuck you!" a light-skinned man sitting closest to him said, causing the others to howl harder in laughter.

"Fuck you, Quan," Tracy said and scooped Vy up over his shoulder.

He carried her to the back room, and Diana watched helplessly. There was no way her father would ever allow any of his girls to be treated like that. She didn't even know how Tracy had gotten to her, unless he snatched Vy up the way Robert had done to her.

Quan and the rest of them followed behind Tracy. When the door shut, Diana could only imagine what Vy was about to endure.

"Be happy I'm not letting these niggas do you like that," Robert said and gently stroked the place on Diana's face that he'd just slapped. "But you're too valuable. By now, your daddy knows you're missing, probably has his people scouring the streets looking for you. I think I'm gon' let him sweat it out a little longer before I make my call."

Vy's deafening screams came suddenly from the back room but were quickly followed by a thud. The screaming turned into loud pained cries, and Diana heard a ton of bustling around. Her teeth clenched, and all she wanted to do was go back and save Vy. She didn't even care about what Robert had in store for her at that point. A woman's body was meant to be worshipped and cherished, not torn at by wild beasts.

Vy's cries for help vibrated in Diana's eardrums, and the commotion from the back room distracted her so much that she didn't hear the front door open a second time. Neither did Robert.

"It seems like they're having a good time," Robert taunted.

"You didn't seem like such an evil man when I met you earlier," she told him.

"The one thing your daddy should have taught you was how to spot a shark in the water."

"Well, then I'm surprised that you're not back there with the rest of the sharks."

"I thought I told you earlier, I don't pay for pussy. I don't take it either."

"Well, how noble of you," Diana sneered. "You're going to pay for hurting her."

That time, when Robert smacked her, the blow was so hard that it busted her lip. She tasted the blood on her tongue, but she ignored the sting to glare at him.

"You'll pay," she repeated.

"Who's gon' make me?"

"I have someone in mind."

The menacing voice came from behind Robert. She didn't know who it belonged to, but by the way Robert whipped around, he must have. Diana looked to the dark hallway by the front door and could make out the shadowy figure of a man. It was too dark to make out a face, but when he stepped out of the shadows, Diana was shocked.

The person standing before her, wearing a dark blue floral button-up shirt that was open at the top, wasn't a man at all. He was a teenager. Although he was muscular, he didn't look to be much older than her. It took a few moments for Diana to see that he wasn't alone. Three more men stepped out of the shadows but stayed behind the kid.

"C–Caesar," Robert stammered, and Diana swore she heard him swallow a gulp of saliva. "What are you doing here?"

Caesar? Diana thought. So he was Caesar. He wasn't what she expected, but he wasn't less than either. He was breathtaking. The energy in the whole house had shifted, and Diana took note of how his goons hovered close behind him. Even the way Robert's demeanor had changed just that quick spoke volumes. He had gone from being sure of himself to being meek.

Caesar stared at Robert for a while with icy eyes before he looked down the hallway behind Diana. Vy's screams had subsided, but there was still a lot of movement going on back there.

"Did you just ask me what I'm doing in my own spot?" His question came out blandly.

"Nah, that's not what I meant, boss. I just wasn't expecting you."

"Always expect me. Especially when I find out a house of mine is being used when it isn't supposed to be," Caesar said as his eyes finally rested on Diana. "Everything good here?"

"Yeah," Robert said quickly. "She's just—"

"Domino Reyes' daughter." Caesar cut him off and gave him a look that dared him to lie.

"Yes," Robert said.

"It wasn't a question. I know who she is. What I want to know is why is she in my spot?"

"I—"

"Matter of fact, shut the fuck up." Caesar cut him off again, and Robert did just that. "I can guess why she's here. You saw her father earlier at the party I set up for you ungrateful muthafuckas. Maybe she was with him and you saw her as a quick come up. You're holding her as ransom."

When he was done speaking, he nodded his head once, and one of the men behind him went down the hallway, while the other two went toward Robert. One of them grabbed him by the arms and stood back, while the other punched him hard in the gut twice. He doubled over, but Caesar threw his head back up.

Watching the scene in front of her, Diana put two and two together. Robert had lied.

"I didn't order this," Caesar said, confirming Diana's thoughts. "We just got done fighting with the Asians. Now you're starting shit with the Dominicans?"

"You don't pay us shit, man!" Robert stated. "Ever since your pops died, shit ain't been the same. That nigga kept money in our pockets, but you seem to just be keeping money in yours!"

On his last word, Caesar's goon punched him in his jaw so hard that Diana saw blood fly. Before he could completely regain his wits, Caesar grabbed Robert by the chin and forced him to look into his eyes.

"You must have forgotten about the tyranny my father left behind. If the only reason we eat is because we are starving out others, how good is the food really? This is chess, not checkers, and the shit I have in motion, everybody is going to feast like kings. You have no idea what you've just done. And you used my name and resources to do it."

Caesar let his chin go when his goon brought the men who were in the back room up front. They were in their shirts and underwear. They had looks of regret on their faces when they saw Caesar glaring at them. Diana noticed that a few of them had smears of red on their shirts, and her arms fought violently against her restraints.

"Untie me. Untie me!" she shouted frantically at the goon who had just brought the men out. She looked behind her at the bedroom door and saw that the door to the room was open, but Vy hadn't come out. *"Fucking untie me!"*

The goon looked to Caesar to get his approval, and Caesar nodded his head. The man undid her bonds, and the moment Diana felt that she was free, she jumped out of the chair and tried to run to the back room. The goon grabbed her and gave her a warning look. She knew what it meant and inhaled deeply through her mouth while fighting back tears.

"No." She shook her head and pulled away.

She readied herself for what she might see when she rushed to the room, but when she got there, she realized there wasn't enough preparation in the world. She stopped abruptly in the doorway and placed a hand over her mouth to stop herself from screaming. Vy was sprawled out on the bed, naked and on her back. Her eyes were closed, and her body was completely still. It was her face that turned Diana's stomach. Her jaw looked as though it had been broken, and there was wet blood all over her face. Diana dropped her hand and walked slowly to the bed and sat down.

"Vy," she whispered, even though she knew Vy wasn't going to answer.

Vy wasn't breathing. She was dead. It was the first time Diana had been so close to a dead body, and surprisingly, there was no fear inside of her. In fact, there was nothing. Just numbness. She kept running the chain of events through her head and trying to figure out if there was *anything that she could have done differently. All she could think of was earlier when she was in the car and she saw how uncomfortable Vy looked. Diana wished she would have said something to her dad about it. He could have done something.*

"I'm sorry," she said and left the room. She went back to the living room and gave Caesar a blank stare. "She's dead."

"I know," Caesar told her and sighed. "They crossed the line. You can present them to your father, and he can figure out what to do with them."

Diana nodded. That was the sensible thing to do. It was the right thing to do. But it wasn't what she wanted to do. The numbness she felt was subsiding. Rage was replacing it. Pure rage. Her body seemed to move and have a mind of its own when she grabbed Caesar's gun from his waist. She cocked it and turned it on the men who had caused her chest to ache. She tugged the trigger repeatedly, causing loud bangs to sound, but she barely heard them. All she was focused on were the neat holes that formed in the middle of their foreheads. Two of them tried to run, but her bullets caught them in the back of their necks. Lastly, she turned the gun on Robert.

"Fuck you, bitch," he said. "Go ahead and kill me."

"After you suffer," she told him, aimed the gun at his crotch, and fired.

He screamed loudly, his knees buckled, and he dropped to the ground. She watched him writhe on the floor in pain, holding his dick. Diana hoped she'd blown it off.

"Don't worry. You weren't going to be able to use it again anyway," she told him.

Before he could muster out any more curses at her, she emptied the clip in his face. She kept squeezing the trigger, even after there were no bullets left.

She breathed heavily, and when it dawned on her that she had murdered five people, she handed Caesar his gun. His goons looked at her incredulously, almost as if they couldn't believe that she had the heart to do what she had just done. But not Caesar.

"Feel better?" he asked.

"No," she answered honestly. "I want to go home."

"I'll take her," one of Caesar's goons said, but Caesar shook his head.

"Nah, Jo, I'll take her. Her father is going to need to speak with me."

"Then we'll follow you."

"Just go to my house and wait for me. I'll be straight."

There was a deafening silence that took over the room as they looked at each other. Diana could tell that they didn't want to let Caesar go alone. They cared about him. No, they respected him. It was a wild sight to see how they took orders from him and how they never made a move without his okay.

"I'll tell my papá what really happened," Diana said, breaking the silence. "He's a good man. He will be angry at first, but in the end, he will be grateful that you saved my life."

"I won't even need you to do that. Come on. My car is outside."

"But what about Vy?"

"I'll have someone clean up in here. I'll also make sure she has a nice funeral. But trust me when I say you don't

want to stay in here too much longer. It's going to start stinking soon."

Diana glanced back at the room before nodding and following Caesar out the front door. The sky was dark and filled with stars. Diana had no idea what time it was, but she could assume it was late. She could only imagine the kind of panic that her father was in.

Caesar's sandy brown BMW was parked on the street, and when they got to it, he opened her car door. She got in and sat down on the white leather seat and inhaled the citrus scent coming from the car freshener.

When Caesar got in the car, she pulled the visor down and took a look at her face. There was dried blood on her lip that she licked and wiped away. The back of her head was still aching, and the right side of her face was slightly swollen, but she would take that over the way that she'd left Robert. She closed the visor, not wanting to see herself like that anymore, and told Caesar her address.

"You don't feel nothing?" Caesar asked after a few minutes of driving.

"My head is hurting a little bit, but other than that I'm all right."

"That's not what I meant," Caesar said, taking his eyes off the road to look over at her. "You just killed five people."

"I know what I did. And I would do it again," she told him.

"Have you ever murdered anyone before?"

"No. But they crossed a line that should have never been crossed." Her voice was soft as she spoke. "The truth is, my papá would have paid any dollar amount to get me back. I know this because we are all we have. It's *been just us two since my mother died five years ago. I am his light, and he is my shield. When I heard Robert say that he was going to kill me anyway, I couldn't bear the thought of leaving my papá with that pain. So, Robert had to die for even trying to do that to him. My papá says that people are always left with their first impression of you. And I want people to know not to ever fuck with me. What happened to me today will never happen again."*

"The biggest lessons come from if you live to tell the tale of a mistake," Caesar said.

Diana didn't know why, but it made her laugh.

"What?"

"It's just funny to hear words like that come from the mouth of a teenager. You can't be that much older than me."

"I'll be nineteen soon, but age in these streets don't matter. Heart matters."

"See, you did it again." Diana giggled and then grew serious. "What were you talking about back there? The things you were saying to Robert, about everybody eating."

"Oh, that," Caesar said and sighed. "Shit is getting too dangerous out here. If I don't do something soon, there will only be scraps left for everybody. I'm tired of fighting over work and territory. Everybody feels entitled to everything, and shit never works out for the better that way. We're all stepping on each other's toes—my family, your family, the Asians, the Mexicans, the Italians, and the other Blacks. We run New York. We need to come together and stop feuding with each other. Every time one war ends between a family, another starts. I'm calling for a cease fire."

"Yeah, and who is going to listen to that?"

"They all will."

"And how do you know that?"

"Because my family is the only one out of all that has never lost a war. Everyone that has stood against us has lost. They'll listen because I won't give them any other choice."

Diana came back to the present again and placed Caesar's hand back on the bed beside his body. Her father had been her first example of what a real man was, but Caesar was for sure the second. The first time he met her, he saved her life. For that, she owed him her undying loyalty. And not just for just that, but for years later when her father died.

Because she was his only child and a girl, everyone thought his empire should go to her first cousin, Dupree. They didn't think she could do the job. Caesar stepped in and called for a vote, and after that, she was tested to see if she could do the job. It was much like the vote she called for Boogie. She would never forget that. Nor would she forget that someone so young was the one who united them all.

Diana stood to her feet and kissed him on his forehead before placing her lips by his ear. "You didn't give them another choice, and now I'm not giving you any other choice," she whispered as if he could hear her. She hoped he could. "Pull through, Caesar. We need you."

"I'm going to make some calls and see if anybody knows anything about this shit," Marco was saying when she stood back up.

"Me too. Maybe one of my clients knows something," Diana said, speaking of her high-paying tricks.

One thing about being in the business of selling pussy was that men often weaponized their money and knowledge. A lot of times, they talked too much, trying to impress the beautiful women in their company. Those same women came back and told Diana everything, the things they said, and even their filthiest fetishes. In fact, blackmail was how Diana had formed alliances with some very powerful people.

"Li, see if anybody in Chinatown has been saying anything," she said, and he nodded. "We have to find out who has a target on our heads."

Chapter 4

Not wanting to let too much time pass between everyone finding out about Caesar's untimely death and his journey to the top, Boogie hopped on the opportunity train, with the first stop being in Staten Island. Smoothly, he parked his Lamborghini outside of an old run-down butchery and stepped cockily out of the vehicle. His newly appointed right-hand man, Bentley, got out of the passenger's seat. Both were in regular street gear and wore menacing looks on their faces.

"You ready to do this?" Bentley asked when both of their feet graced the sidewalk.

"Yup," Boogie answered.

Boogie had filled Bentley in on all of the recent events and what Caesar had done. He also told Bentley his next course of action and what he planned to do. Boogie gave him the option to take the money they'd made together on their last heist and be done with it all. He said he wouldn't hold it against him.

"Hell nah. If you're rockin', I'm rollin', and that's just that on that," was what Bentley had replied.

Bentley had been shocked to find out the news behind Barry's killer, but he was ready to stand ten toes behind Boogie through whatever. So, when Boogie told him that he walked away from the other four families and was ready to take over everything, Bentley was ready to go. Boogie had proven himself to be a friend, and Bentley's mind was on how much more money they could get together. That morning was just the beginning.

The two of them entered and walked through the dimly lit building. The sound of their footsteps echoed all around them, and Boogie took note of how badly it smelled. He looked around and saw that some of the butcher's equipment was still lying around, and there were some dark stains dried on the floor under where he assumed the animals would hang.

"This place gives me the creeps, yo," Bentley noted as they walked.

"I think that's the point," Boogie said. "Bring a nigga through a butchery and he'll be shakin' in his boots by the time he reaches you. All he's gon' be thinkin' about is torture."

They finally found an elevator in the back and got on it. It only went down, so Boogie pressed the button and let it take them to the lower level of the building. When it stopped and the doors opened, they got off and realized they were now in a long and wide hallway. At the end of the hall was an open door, and there were voices coming from behind it. In the distance, it sounded as if a heated discussion was going on. Boogie checked his surroundings and got off the elevator first. He'd noticed how easy it had been to get down there. Nobody had even tried to stop them. He kept his hand close to his hip just in case someone tried to spring out at them.

He and Bentley walked side by side until they reached the entrance of a big room, where they came face to face with a group of Italian men who seemed shocked to see the newcomers and didn't react right away. Still, Boogie held his hand close to his gun. The men glowered at them.

It was apparent that they weren't welcome. That didn't stop Bentley from being obnoxious.

"Yo, what the fuck happened here?" Bentley asked, looking around. His eyes went to the bullet holes in the walls and then to the ones in the pool table. "It looks like an episode of *Gangland* up in here."

Boogie had to agree. Although the carpet was red, he could see that some spots were a darker red than others. He knew a blood stain when he saw one.

"There was obviously a disagreement." A voice spoke from behind the Italians.

They cleared the way so that he could pass. When Boogie saw who it was, he furrowed his brow and brandished his pistol. He stopped himself from pulling the trigger when he aimed the gun, but Lord knew he wanted to empty the clip. Ohio's kingpin, Shamar Hafford, stood before him, looking as smug as ever. He wore a long pea coat over a suit and a fedora hat on his head.

"What are you doing here?" Boogie asked through his teeth.

"The same thing you are. Attempting to set up shop," Shamar answered.

"You're one bold motherfucka to show your face around town. Especially after all you've done."

"Well, I guess I'm just a bold motherfucka then. Also, I could say the same to you, being that you *are* the man that murdered my son," Shamar replied distastefully.

"Shit happens when shit ain't supposed to be happenin', if you catch my drift." Boogie shrugged.

"Maybe you're right," Shamar said, giving Boogie an almost humorous look. "Come have a drink with me."

"I'm still stuck on you saying that you're here to set up shop, because I hope you know that's not gon' ever shake."

"And why wouldn't it?" Shamar asked. "The way I see it, this territory is up for grabs. And it's clear that these muthafuckas don't know what the hell they're doing without Bosco."

"Nigga, you ain't even from New York tryna stake claim," Boogie commented, twisting his face up.

"You're right." Shamar smirked. "The truth is a little birdie told me that I'd be able to find you here. And well, here you are."

Some of the Italian men in the room swiveled their heads, looking from Boogie to Shamar. It was apparent by the looks of distaste on their faces that they weren't feeling the conversation.

One of them stepped away from the rest and pointed at Boogie. "Who the hell said that either of you would be setting up shop here? This is our shit!"

Boogie eyed him down. He was an older man who was dressed suave, clean cut from his head to his chin. He had stepped away from the others, so that he was in the fold with the newcomers. Boogie wondered if he was their new self-appointed leader. If he was, then he was about to be in for a rude awakening.

"What's your name?" Boogie asked.

"Jesse."

"Well, Jesse, word on the street is y'all had something to do with Caesar's death."

"Well, word on the street would be wrong. That crazy motherfucka came in here starting shit with us. Ask him. He was here when he killed Bosco."

Jesse jabbed a thumb at Shamar, and that *was* news to Boogie. Shamar had the look of a child caught with his hand in the cookie jar. Boogie had to admit, Shamar being there at all was questionable. How did he and Bosco connect at all?

"We'll come back to that," Boogie said, letting his gaze linger on Shamar for a second before turning back to Jesse. "So, you mean to tell me that you had nothin' to do with Caesar's death?"

"If we did, we'd be singing that tune from here to the high heavens. Especially after how he did Bosco."

Boogie couldn't lie. He was confused at that point. If they hadn't killed Caesar, then who had? He shook the thought away, not wanting to let the befuddlement show on his face. Caesar had probably made a lot of enemies during his reign at the top. One of them might have just caught up to him.

"How unfortunate," was all Boogie said and motioned his hands around the room. "Well, I'm happy to be the one to inform you that this is my shit now. I'll be expectin' a grand tour soon."

"Over my dead body," Jesse sneered.

"We can make that happen, muthafucka." Bentley rushed forward, jabbing his gun to Jesse's dome. He cocked it and pressed the weapon hard against Jesse's temple. Both men glared at each other, but Jesse didn't dare move a muscle. Boogie's eyes went from him to the rest of the Italians.

"You can come the easy way or the hard way. But *either* way, you and I both know that you don't have the power to go against me. I'm offering you an opportunity to work under me. If you don't take it and try to fight me, your families will pay the price. Your mothers, your fathers, your siblings, and your children. I will break you down until you are a fraction of the man you once were, by takin' away everything you love. By the time I kill your body, you would have already been dead inside."

"You don't have the stomach," Jesse spat. "I know all about you. You're Barry's boy. The chef! We used to laugh with Bosco about you. You ain't no killer."

Boogie didn't feel like he had to fall into that tough guy role to appease them. He was just tired of hearing the Italian's mouth. So when he pulled out his own Glock, it was more to shut Jesse up than to prove a point. His gun barked three times, and the force of the bullets snapped Jesse's head back and opened up his chest. He fell at the feet of his friends, and they could barely hide the worrisome expressions on their faces, watching him bleed out on the floor, dead.

They seemed like they wanted to do something. After all, there were more of them, but Bentley's gun pointed their way made them rethink those actions. Also, there was something about the sinister look Boogie gave each of them that made them not want to see how far he would go. Jesse had been wrong; Boogie was a killer. Little did they know, the old Boogie would have never just killed someone in cold blood like that. But in a short time, something inside of him had changed. His heart was cold, and he was willing to do whatever to get what he wanted, even if it meant eradicating the Italians completely out of Staten Island.

"Anybody else have anything smart to say?" Boogie asked, letting the hand holding the gun drop to his side. "Or are you ready to get back to work? I don't want to have to target your families, but I will. We can continue makin' a profit together, and what I have to offer is more money than any of you ever made under Bosco."

One of them spoke up. "How can you offer that if we still have to work in this one territory?"

"That's where you're wrong," Boogie told him. "Expansion is comin'."

"The other families won't allow it."

"What's your name?"

"Ralph," the man answered.

"Well, Ralph, I guess it's good for you that we're gettin' rid of the other families and the pact," Boogie said, and from the corner of his eyes, he saw Shamar's brows raise. "With Caesar dead, the others are weak. It's only a matter of time before his own faction starts feuding from within. Now is the time to strike and forever sit at the top. I know you're tired of being thrown scraps, so I'm here to offer a feast."

Ralph turned to the others, and when they nodded at him, he averted his gaze back to Boogie.

"It might work."

"It will work," Boogie corrected him. "Our families joined together will be somethin' that nobody expects. And when we're done, you won't have to outsource. You can do business anywhere in New York."

"As long as we answer to you," Ralph said, making Boogie smirk. "You want to be the man in charge. Even bigger than Caesar was."

"You're catching on, Ralph my boy. Now get the fuck out of here and spread the word that this is my operation now. Oh, and have somebody come get Jesse before he starts stinkin'."

Ralph nodded slowly and motioned his head for the others to follow him out of the room. When they were gone, only Boogie, Bentley, and Shamar were left standing. Boogie waved his gun toward the bar and went to sit on one of the stools. Shamar followed suit, while Bentley stood behind them with his gun still drawn. Boogie set his Glock on the bar top and poured himself a glass of brandy, not bothering to ask Shamar if he wanted any.

"Give me one reason why I should let you walk out of that door with your life," Boogie asked, swirling the liquor around the glass.

"If you wanted to kill me, I suspect I'd already be dead," Shamar answered, clasping his hands together. "Ask me what you want to know."

"Why were you here the day Bosco was murdered?"

"We were discussing business."

"Tell me somethin'. How does somebody like you and somebody like Bosco get in cahoots?"

"I'm sure you know by now that this is a market that I've been interested in. So it shouldn't come as a shock that I was doing business with somebody here."

"It still doesn't make sense why that somebody was Bosco. What did he offer you?"

Shamar chuckled but didn't say anything. Instead, he reached for a bottle of vodka next to him. He poured himself a shot and threw it back. His silence was golden.

"You slimy muthafucka. You were plannin' your own takeover, huh? Was all the noise Shane made just a distraction for that?"

"Oh, on the contrary. The beef you had with my son was real. He was always a hothead and never seemed to do a job right. While he was here, he was supposed to stay under the radar, but even that was too much like right for him. The irony is that he died at your hand, and here I am doing business with you."

"Slow your roll. Ain't nobody said anything about doin' business with you."

"But you should."

"And why is that?"

"Are you expecting to go to war with the other families with just the Italians and him?" Shamar shot Bentley a glance and laughed.

"I can make that smile permanent if you want," Bentley threatened.

"Oh no, trust me. I like my face just the way it is," Shamar told him, clearly still amused.

"I have my whole borough backing me," Boogie said, responding to his comment.

"And you think that will be enough going up against three? Caesar may be dead, but his empire is very much alive. I know you're counting on them fighting amongst each other, but what if they don't? You better check your history, boy, just like I did before I made a move on New York. Nobody has ever gone up against Caesar's empire and won. So them, plus the other families, ha! They'll demolish you. Let me walk out of here alive, and I can provide you with the manpower that will bring you a victory."

"Nah, that's too easy. What's in it for you?" Boogie asked, knowing there had to be a catch.

"Well, I want a territory, of course," Shamar said simply. "Caesar's, to be exact."

"And I should take this deal over killin' you because?"

"Because you want to see me dead far less than you want to see yourself reach your objective. And I'm the man who can help you do it."

Boogie mulled over his words. As much as he hated to admit it, Shamar was right. He needed more manpower if he was going to win the budding war. But he didn't trust Shamar as far as he could throw him. He would have to think about the proposition. Boogie took a swig of his drink and took the burning sensation in his throat like a man.

"Leave your number," he said, placing the glass back on the bar top. "I'll be in touch."

Shamar pulled a pen out of the breast pocket of his coat and wrote a number down on a napkin. He then slid it over to Boogie and stood up from the barstool. Tipping his hat, he made his exit.

"I just have one question," Bentley asked, sitting down in the place Shamar was once seated.

"Why should we trust him?"

"Nah," Bentley said, looking seriously into Boogie's face. "Where the fuck was all them niggas parked at? Because I ain't see one car out front!"

Boogie laughed into his glass and downed his drink. When it was gone, he set the glass down and looked around the room. There was a lot of work that needed to be done. Bullet holes didn't make for good décor.

"This is our shit now," he said. "We'll learn the ins and outs soon. Call Tazz and have him come down here and set up shop. We don't have any time to waste."

After Boogie dropped Bentley off later on that day, he couldn't deny the fact that he needed some TLC. There was only one person who could give him that. His girlfriend, Roz, swung the front door of her house open before Boogie had even parked his car. Her daughter, Amber, was sitting on her hip with a cookie in her hand. The way they smiled big at just the sight of him instantly put his mind at ease. He got out of the SUV and grinned as he approached them.

"Gimme this," he said and acted like he was about to take the cookie away from Amber.

She snatched away from him in a fit of giggles. She was wearing a Fendi outfit that he'd recently bought her, and it already had red juice stains in the front of it. Roz had kept telling him not to spend so much money on her clothes because she wasn't going to do anything but mess them up, but he didn't care. He wanted his baby girl to be draped in the best of the best. His baby girl. That was how he had been viewing her as of late. The more time he spent with them, the more he couldn't see his life without them in it. He smiled at Amber and she puckered her lips up at him.

"Mah!" she said. It was her way of letting him know that she wanted a kiss, but he shook his head.

"I gotta get cleaned up first before I let either one of you kiss me," he said, and Roz stepped out of the way so that he could come inside.

"Long day at work?" she asked, piercing him with her light brown eyes.

"Hell yeah. I had to handle some business," Boogie said, taking off his coat.

"Mm-hmm," Roz said, giving him a quizzical look. "That better be the reason why you're showering as soon as you come in this house. Let me find out you were out here steppin' with one of these bitches. She gon' die, and you gon' be hurt really, really bad."

"So much violent talk in front of the baby." Boogie shook his head. "You know you're the only one for me, girl. I wouldn't have did all this if I was just gon' dog you out."

"You better keep it that way," Roz told him, and then spoke in a baby voice to Amber. "Tell him he better keep it that way because yo' mama don't play that! No, she don't." She bounced Amber on her hip, making her laugh again before heading to her bedroom in back. It was then that Boogie took note of the two-piece maroon track suit she was wearing with her Gucci slippers. It hugged her hourglass shape and cupped her booty perfectly.

"Where'd you get that from?" Boogie asked, following behind her.

"Get what?" she asked, glancing back and seeing his eyes were on her bottom. "Oh, this outfit? Some online boutique. I can't remember the name."

"Well, figure it out and order five more of them joints in different colors," he told her, making her giggle.

"You like it?"

"Hell yeah. So much that I can't wait to take it off you so you can save it for a different day." He licked his lips at her as she switched inside Amber's room.

"Well, wait until I put her to sleep, then you can help me preserve my clothing." She winked at him.

Boogie let her do her mom thing while he went to the master bedroom and hopped in the shower. None of Jesse's blood had gotten on him, but he still felt like he was filthy from the job. Boogie scrubbed his entire body ten times before finally getting out. He dried himself off and moisturized his body real good. He wiped the fog from the mirror and looked at himself through the smear his hand had made. His thoughts were empty as he stared at himself. He didn't know what he was looking for, so he couldn't find it. Clenching his jaw slightly, he opened the bathroom door to go put on some underwear.

"Unh-uh." He heard Roz come up behind him when he tried to get his under garments out of his designated drawer. "What you need those for when you can wear me?"

He smiled when he felt her full, heart-shaped lips kissing his back. She wrapped her arms around him, placing one hand on his six pack while the other wrapped around his third leg. It jumped to attention at the first feel of her soft hands, and she stroked it gently.

"Turn around," she whispered.

When he did, he saw she was already naked. She stood on the tips of her toes to kiss him deeply, and their tongues enveloped each other. His hands caressed her smooth skin and fondled her full breasts. Soon, the passionate kiss turned to one of hunger, and he felt his dick grow rock hard. She was the only woman who had ever been able to make him so horny from just a kiss.

She felt him pressing against her and broke away from him. "Don't worry. You can get one too," she said, dropping to her knees.

She wrapped her lips around his tip and sucked while swiveling her tongue all around it. He moaned loudly and moved her hair out of her face when she slid the tip all the way to the back of her throat and did a swallow motion. Her mouth was so wet and warm, his dick felt like it was at home. She began slurping and swallowing on him so good that he had to lean against the dresser for support, otherwise his knees were going to give in.

"Fuck baby," he breathed. "Let me get some pussy before you make me nut."

Roz deep-throated him a few more times before she took it out of her mouth and kissed it. She knew what he wanted before he had to ask, and she assumed the face down, ass up position on the bed.

Her round peach was looking good enough to eat, and that's exactly what Boogie did. He put his entire face in it, letting his tongue glide continuously from her pretty asshole to in between her fat pussy lips. He let her wetness build up before he attacked her clit from behind. He put the whole thing in his mouth and sucked while constantly flicking his tongue. When she started quivering, he placed his arms on the arch of her back to hold her in place so he could finish his meal.

"Bryshon!" she cried out. "Baby, I can't take it. I'm about to cummmm!"

Boogie heard the sound of the sheets being snatched from the corners of the bed, and he knew it was because she was gripping them tightly. He kept sucking until he felt the sweet nectar from her orgasm come down, and when it did, he stood up and shoved his thick nine inches of meat deep inside of her. The side of her face was mushed into the bed, and her eyes rolled in the back of her head while he stroked her mercilessly. He felt another wave of her juices squirt out on his torso, and knew he was giving it to her right. Her walls clenched tightly around his shaft and massaged his tip so good that he had to moan.

"Oh, fuck, Roz. This pussy feels so good," he complimented her.

It was only the second time they'd had sex, and it felt even better than the first time. And that first time was explosive. While he watched her ass twerk and continuously swallow his meat, he couldn't help but to grab handfuls. Suddenly, that position became too much for him. He pulled out and flipped her on her back, otherwise he knew he was going to cum quick.

Pulling her to the edge of the bed, Boogie gripped the front of her thighs as he slid back into her. That position was worse. All he saw was her pretty face twisted up in pleasure and her chocolatey brown nipples bouncing with each thrust. He knew it was only a matter of time before he erupted, but he wanted her to cum at least one more time.

As he dove deeply in and out of her love tunnel, Boogie massaged her engorged clit to stimulate a faster orgasm. While doing so, he also began sensually sucking the toes on one of her feet. Soon, he saw her trembling on the bed and felt her walls contracting around his dick. Her back arched like she was possessed without warning, and her juices shot out all over him.

It was over for him at that point. He snatched himself out of her just in time and masturbated his own nut out on her stomach. His body jerked at how powerful his own climax was, and when he was done, he couldn't do anything but fall onto the bed beside her.

They both lay there in silence, trying to catch their breath. After some time had passed, Boogie felt Roz get up from the bed and go to the bathroom. When she did that, he turned his body and moved his head up by the pillows. He laid on his back and put one of his arms over his head and waited for her to come back to bed. When she did, she placed her head on his chest and scooted close to him.

"Something tells me that you really needed that," she said.

"I did."

"I can tell. That was a lot of nut." She laughed, and he did too.

"You workin' some kind of magic on me, shorty," he said, kissing her forehead. "You turn me on in every way."

The room went silent again for a while, and Boogie allowed himself to get lost in his own head. The moment he'd just shared with Roz was just a temporary escape from the world, but soon enough, everything came flooding back at the forefront of his thoughts. He didn't like the idea of going into business with Shamar. Beside the fact that he'd already proven himself to be a foe, there was something else about him that didn't sit well with Boogie. Still, he needed him.

Quiet as it was kept, Boogie had been wondering how he would go head-to-head with all four of the other families. Even with the Italians on his side, he would have had to go to war with each family one by one, and he knew they wouldn't let that happen. He felt like he had no choice but to work with Shamar. He would just have to be careful.

"So . . ." Roz interrupted his thoughts and looked up at him as if she were searching for something.

"So what?" he asked.

"You gon' tell me what's on your mind?"

Boogie sighed. He didn't want to bring Roz in it, but by being his girl, she was already in it. He needed somebody with a level head to talk to.

"Do you really wanna know?"

"I wouldn't have asked if I didn't, Boogie."

"I'm going to war with the other families," he said bluntly.

"What?" Roz sat up, brushing her hair from her face. "You're doing what?"

"Caesar killed my father."

"And he's dead now," Roz told him like that should be the end of it.

"Nah, you don't get it. Caesar went against his own pact, so why should I follow it? I'm not gon' live by the rules he set in place anymore. I stepped away from the table."

"But . . . what does that mean for everything else?"

"It means that soon they're going to try and confine me to one area the same way they did the Italians. And I'm not gon' let them. Diana keeps tryna contact me, but I'm done with all that shit. Caesar took more from me than he knows, so I'm about to take everything that once was his, plus everything else."

"Baby," Roz said and placed her hand on his chest. "I understand you're angry, but think about what you're doin'."

"I have thought about it!" Boogie barked a little more aggressively than he intended to.

"All I'm sayin' is that maybe you should meet with the other families. Maybe there is a peaceful resolution."

"Yeah? Like what?"

"I don't know. Maybe you should pick up the phone and see." She turned her back on him and got under the messed-up covers. "But I'm going to try and get some sleep before Amber wakes back up. I was thinking steak sounds good for dinner."

"Yeah, that's straight," Boogie said, although his mind was still on her words.

He'd wanted to talk to somebody sensible and didn't know why he was angry that he'd gotten some sensible advice. What she had said truly wasn't what he wanted to hear.

He sighed and reached for his phone. He typed out a text message to Diana, asking her when she wanted to meet. A minute after sending the message, he got one back. He read it before tossing his phone to the side and closing his eyes.

Chapter 5

Diana found herself subconsciously checking the diamond-studded watch on her wrist. She was sitting at the round table in her normal chair at the normal meeting place, but everything felt different. There were only three of them, and where they were seated made it feel like they were so spaced out. She kept glancing over at Caesar's chair and thinking about him laid up helpless in that bed. Something had to be done.

The day before, she'd finally gotten a hold of Boogie, and he agreed to meet. He was supposed to be there at two o'clock in the afternoon, and it was now thirty minutes past that. However, she was still holding onto the hope that he would show.

The whole time they were waiting, Diana kept asking herself what Caesar would do. Then she reminded herself that she couldn't go about it the way Caesar would have, because Caesar would have respected Boogie's wishes to walk away, while Diana couldn't. She figured Boogie was just frustrated and needed time to blow off some steam.

"Where the hell is this kid?" Marco asked, looking at the clock on the wall.

"Just give him some more time. He'll be here," Diana assured him.

The words had barely left her mouth when finally one of the double doors to the meeting room swung open. In came Boogie with a whole entourage behind him. There was a new kind of swagger about him that Diana couldn't quite put her finger on. His aura was just different, and it could be felt throughout the room. It was cocky almost. Diana's brow raised slightly, and she and Li exchanged glances.

"When a meeting time is agreed upon, it is formal to be punctual," she said, letting Boogie know she didn't appreciate his late arrival.

"I only move when my drum beats," Boogie responded, and Diana was taken aback.

"Please have your men wait outside the door," Marco told him.

Diana recognized some of them as men that worked under Barry. Tazz, Barry's nephew, was one of them. Even he seemed to have a harder look about him.

"Where I am, they are," Boogie said simply.

"That is not and will never be the protocol," Diana told him in an even tone. "Tell them to wait outside. I won't ask again."

Tazz looked at Boogie, who finally nodded, before he led the others out of the room. When they were gone and the door was closed once again, Boogie took a seat. That time, however, he didn't sit in Barry's seat. He sat in Caesar's. Marco opened his mouth to say something about it, but Diana put a hand up to stop him.

"Boogie, I'm glad you could make it despite your tardiness," she said.

"To what do I owe this summoning?" he asked, clasping his hands on the table.

"If I remember right, you reached out to me," Diana told him.

"Only because you kept callin'. We can either go back and forth on who was more thirsty for who, or we can get down to business."

There was a time when he was just a boy that she could give him one piercing gaze and he would lower his head. But right then, the one she gave him didn't even make him waver. Something in him had changed. The man he was then and the man he was a month ago were two completely different people. He was harder . . . colder. She blinked and cleared her throat.

"We fear that we're at war," she started. "With your father being murdered and Caesar—"

"Actually before you finish your sentence, let me go ahead and ask this. Did the rest of you know that Caesar killed my father?"

"W–what?" Diana asked incredulously. "What are you talking about, Boogie?"

"Exactly what I just said. I hope your shock is sincere and not an act, because I'm already pretty pissed off."

"Caesar didn't kill Barry. That's a ridiculous claim!"

"I know he did, and he killed Julius too. I also find it odd how all the footage at Big Wheels mysteriously vanished."

"Then how do you know for certain what happened? I know you're still hurting behind Barry, but making false claims won't make that pain go away."

"He did! I saw him standin' over Unc, holdin' the gun he killed him with. It was still smokin'."

Diana knew that Julius had been murdered in the same place Caesar was found. She didn't know what had happened, and she didn't want to jump to conclusions either. However, she just guessed that whoever had gotten to Caesar had gotten to Julius too. She never once thought that Caesar had been the one to do it. That was troublesome to her, but now something else was on her mind.

"You were at Big Wheels the night Caesar was murdered?" Diana asked, but her true question was in her tone.

"Yeah, I was there, but I didn't kill Caesar. I wanted to. God knows I did, but I couldn't. He was still alive when I left. I heard about his death on the news later that night. And I'm glad somebody did it. I just wish they'd given him the same kind of death my father got. Slow and painful."

"Boogie, Caesar didn't kill Barry!" Diana tried to reason with him.

"And how would you know for sure?"

"It just doesn't make sense."

"I know all about the deal he tried to make back in the day that my pops blocked. That was why they fell out."

"That was so long ago. Caesar wouldn't have killed him because of that."

"I know what I saw. What other reason would he have had for killing Julius if it weren't to cover his tracks? I'm sure he would have killed me too eventually."

"Boogie—"

"The only reason I came here today was to see if any of you had anything to do with my father's death," Boogie said and looked at the three of them. "I believe you when you say that you didn't. And because of that, I'm going to give you an option."

"An option?" Li asked. "We brought you here to—"

"Let him speak," Diana cut Li off, and he gave her a mean look, but there was a method to her madness.

"I'm going to give all of you the choice to, as they say, come quietly," Boogie said.

"Come quietly?" Marco scoffed. "What the hell is that supposed to mean, kid?"

"It means I want it all. My territory, Caesar's, and all of yours. The years of the pact have come and gone. It's time for new management."

"And by new management, you mean you?" Li laughed loudly. "This has to be some kind of a joke."

"Do you see me laughing?" Boogie asked with a blank face. "I'll give you until the end of this week to take my offer."

"I don't need a week to tell you to go to hell. I'll never give up my territory to you," Marco told him.

"Me either," Li chimed in.

"I agree. You can't expect us to take you serious, Boogie," Diana said, noticing the tension in the room heating up. "I know you're upset right now, but I'm sure there is something that we can work out businesswise."

"That's not good enough for me. I gave you your option, and that's the only one."

"Or else what?" Marco asked, humoring him.

"If you don't give me what I want, then I'll be forced to take it," Boogie said simply.

It was Diana's turn to laugh. Barry's empire, now Boogie's, was very strong in force, but nowhere near strong enough to take on the likes of four. It would be a massacre. Her laugh subsided, however, when she saw him sitting there looking so sure of himself. It made her curious.

"Nah. Go ahead and keep laughing. All of y'all. Laugh it up," Boogie said and clapped his hands a few times. He connected eyes with Diana. "The only reason I really came to this meeting was because of you. You gave me a chance, so now I'm giving you one. But if you don't back down and give me what I want, you will regret it."

He didn't wait for any of them to respond. He just stood up and made his way toward the exit, ending the meeting on his own accord. He opened the door and walked out, quietly shutting the door behind him.

When he was gone, Marco and Li looked to Diana. She didn't know what they expected her to say, because she really didn't have any words. Never in a million years would she have expected things to turn the way they just had. Boogie had just declared war on all of them. She was glad that she hadn't told him about Caesar's true state, but she didn't know what good that would even serve.

"Do you think Caesar had something to do with Barry's death?" Li asked.

"I already let one person get away with speaking such blasphemy. I won't let another," Diana warned, and Li shut his mouth.

"So what now?" Marco asked.

"He isn't serious," Diana told them. "Even with the Tollivers removed from the fold and Caesar being in limbo, we are still powerful together. He's bluffing."

"Either way, Boogie needs to be dealt with," Marco stated.

"I agree," Li agreed.

"And how do you suggest we deal with him?" Diana asked.

"The same way we have handled any other threat in the past," Marco said.

"Are you saying that we should kill Barry's son, Marco?" Diana asked so he could clarify.

"I'm saying that we do what we've done to everyone else that was a threat in the past."

"I think we should give him some time," she told them. "We owe Barry that much. After all, how much of a threat could Boogie really be?"

At that moment, Marco's phone began ringing. He pulled it from his pocket, and when he saw the name on the screen, he answered on the first ring.

"Speak," he answered, then listened to the caller. "What?"

Diana watched his face fall. Her mind was still on what had just happened at the meeting; however, she couldn't ignore the angered look on Marco's face. Something must have happened at one of his shops.

"I'm on the way. Tighten up security everywhere!" He hung up the phone and stood to his feet.

"What's wrong?" Diana asked.

"You sure Boogie was just bluffing?" Marco asked as he put his coat on in a hurry. "One of my buildings was just bombed. He killed ten of my men."

As Diana drove home from the meeting, it felt like her car was driving itself. She knew where she was going, but the reason behind it seemed so surreal. The building of Marco's that was attacked was a warehouse where he stored all of his newly imported weapons. Boogie's message had been received.

It was six in the evening when Diana pulled her car to a stop outside of Caesar's home. She went to the door and rang the doorbell. The wind blew at her hair, and she placed her hands in her long coat to keep them warm. Diana hoped someone was home and would open the door soon.

Just as she was about to head back to her car, she heard the lock turn, and the door swung open. Standing there looking confused to see Diana was Caesar's daughter, Milli. She was the spitting image of both Caesar and his ex-wife, and she was as pretty as can be. She was wearing a long-sleeved black dress that stopped just above her knees. She checked behind Diana as if to see if she was alone.

"Auntie Diana," Caesar's daughter, Milli, said when she opened the door. "What are you doing here?"

"I came to see if you knew where I could find Nicky," Diana said, speaking of Caesar's nephew.

Nicky was technically Caesar's little cousin, but the age difference was so wide that Caesar just called him his nephew. He was only in his early thirties and high in rank. One thing about Nicky was that when it came down to it, he was really going to pull it out and murder anything and anybody behind his family. Not only that, but he was smart too. If anybody was going to be in charge of Caesar's empire while he was down, it would be him.

"Nicky? He's actually inside right now," Milli said and tucked her long box braids behind her ears. "Do you want to come in?"

"Yes, please."

Milli stepped out of the way and granted Diana access to the foyer of the mansion. It had been a while since Diana had been there, but not much had changed. Caesar had always enjoyed the finer things in life, and his home was just one example. She'd always admired the crystal chandeliers on his high ceilings, so much so that she'd had similar ones installed in her own home. The marble tile on the floors was new, and it gave the home an even more elegant look.

In the distance, Diana heard the sound of voices, and she smelled the amazing aroma of food being cooked.

"We were having a repast for my father," Milli said with a smile, but Diana heard the sadness in her voice. "We had him cremated. It made sense given the way they found him. No funeral, just a bunch of us remembering the good times. We wanted to pay some sort of respect to him."

Diana forced a smile to her lips and nodded. She hadn't taken into account how hard it would be to lie to Milli's face. Milli thought her father was dead, when in fact he was alive. He might have been fighting for his life, but he was alive.

Milli motioned for Diana to follow and led her to the back of the house. They passed a dining room that was filled with a small party of men and women, who were also wearing all black. Upon seeing Diana, they nodded their heads toward her with respect. Caesar's family knew exactly who she was and knew what kind of weight her name carried. She nodded back and kept following Milli.

When finally they reached a game room with a big TV, couches, and a pool table, they stopped. Diana spotted Nicky sitting on the couch with a few of his other cousins and a fifth of Remy in his hands. He looked distraught, and Diana already knew why. So many people looked up to Caesar. Even though it was a fact that everybody died one day, nobody had expected Caesar to leave so soon. The truth about it all burned at the back of her throat like a consistent cough.

"Auntie Diana?" Milli asked.

"Yes, my love?"

"Are you here because of something about my dad?"

Diana wanted to tell her yes, but just like she hadn't told Boogie a thing, she didn't think anyone needed to know Caesar was still alive. Not until they knew who had tried to kill him. She touched Milli's cheek softly and smiled sadly.

"No, baby," she said, shaking her head. "There is something else that has come up that I need to talk to Nicky about."

"What?"

"Nothing that I would want you to worry your pretty little head about. All I want you to do is to keep honoring your father just like you have been."

"Okay," Milli said and hesitated before she started to leave. "Well, Nicky is over there. Feel free to eat if you're hungry. We have so much food, and I doubt we will eat it all."

"Thank you, baby. I'll be sure to get a plate before I leave."

When Milli was gone, Diana turned her head to Nicky. He hadn't even noticed her enter the large room. Diana walked past the pool table and approached the couch where he was sitting. Seeing a shadow standing over him, Nicky glanced up and saw her looking down at him. His eyes were red, and the tie he wore with his silk black button-up had been loosened. He looked as if he had been going through it.

"We need to talk," she said and motioned for him to come to the small bar in the corner with her.

Nicky passed the bottle to his cousin, who was sitting next to him, and followed Diana. When they were out of earshot of everyone, Diana took Nicky's image in. It was obvious that he was very distraught. He was a handsome young man with smooth brown skin and what the kids called "Pop Smoke" braids in his shoulder-length hair. He was a clean-shaven man except for the mustache above his thick top lip. She could smell the alcohol on him and wondered how long he had been drinking.

"How are you holding up?" she asked.

"I can't believe he's really gone," Nicky said to Diana sadly.

"Me either," she said, still looking him in the eye. "But you know things must continue with or without him."

"I don't think I ever got to tell him what he meant to me. To all of us."

"I'm sure he knew."

"Yeah, I wish we had done more to honor him. He did so much for everybody," Nicky said, looking to the small group of people in the room. "But Milli wanted things to be really close knit."

"I see. She didn't even invite me."

"She's just hurting is all. We all are." Nicky sighed and turned his attention back to her. "I don't need three guesses to figure out why you're here."

"Then you should have an answer for me," Diana said, studying his unsure face.

"I don't know, Diana . . ."

"Nicky, it's inevitable. Somebody has to take Caesar's place right now, and you're next in line. Caesar wouldn't want anybody but you at the forefront of his empire. If it doesn't happen soon, I'm afraid all hell will break out in your camp. Everyone needs management, or business will collapse."

"Isn't there supposed to be some sort of vote?"

"Not this time. Things are . . . different."

"How so?"

"I believe we are about to be at war. All of us."

"War?" Nicky asked in a troubled tone. "With who?"

"Bryshon Tolliver."

"Hold on. That's Barry's son?"

"Yes," Diana responded.

"Wait, wait, wait. Back up," Nicky said, putting his hands up. "Run that shit by me one more time. I thought the families couldn't fight."

"Boogie pulled away from the table. He is not part of us any longer. He . . . he thinks Caesar had something to do with his father's death."

"And did he?"

"No. Or at least I truly don't believe he did. Either way, Caesar is gone, and we have to prepare for the possible threat."

"I mean, how much could he possibly do? It's four against one."

"He just blew up one of Marco's facilities."

"Shit," Nicky said, genuinely shocked. "And Marco's a crazy muthafucka. So Boogie is serious, huh? What do you want me to do, snuff him out and handle him?"

"Eventually. But first I need you to figure out exactly who and what we are dealing with."

"Say no more." Nicky nodded. "I can never be Caesar King, but I can make his legacy proud."

Diana didn't say anything. Instead she cupped his cheek and raised his head slightly. There was a silent exchange that happened between them before she turned and left the room.

She knew she had told Milli that she would grab a plate of food before she left, but in truth, eating was the last thing on her mind. She slipped quietly out of the mansion without being spotted and walked to her car, getting lost in the clicking of her heels against the pavement.

Her thoughts began to consume her. Diana really didn't want to have to hurt Boogie, but she knew if she had to for the greater good of business, she would. There was still one last course of action that she wanted to take to try to defuse the whole situation.

Chapter 6

Ding! Dong!

After the doorbell sounded, Diana once again found herself outside of someone's house, waiting for them to open the door. She'd battled against herself about coming to that specific home. She had stayed away from there longer than she had Caesar's place. At least there, she felt welcome. This time, she knew it would be the opposite.

"Just a second! Here I come!" a pleasant voice called from inside the house.

Diana heard footsteps getting closer to the door, and she prepared herself. She didn't know what kind of reaction she was about to provoke. Still when the door opened, she offered a small smile—small because it was the only kind she could muster.

"Hi, Dina," Diana said.

Dina Tolliver stood wearing a pink jogger suit with her hair pulled in a ponytail. Upon opening the door, she, too, had a smile on her face, but when she saw who was standing outside of her house, that smile quickly faded and turned into a glare.

"Now, what kind of stank-ass wind could have blown the likes of you to my porch?"

"Can we talk?" Diana asked, trying to be nice.

"And why would I want to do something crazy like that?" Dina scoffed. "Do you know where you're at?"

"Yes, I do. And I wouldn't have come if it weren't important."

Dina stared at Diana distastefully for a few more moments before rolling her eyes. She opened the front door all the way and stepped aside so Diana could enter.

The first thing Diana looked for was any sign of Boogie. It was quiet other than the sound of a dishwasher running. The house was exactly how Diana remembered it, minus a few upgrades. The walls were filled with pictures, and the corners of her lips wanted to turn up so bad. Barry had always loved pictures.

Dina took Diana to the home's sitting area, where she already had a glass of tea on the table. She gestured for Diana to take a seat across from her. The two women just stared at each other in silence. Both had aged gracefully, but Dina had a few wrinkles on her face, while Diana did not. Neither had a gray hair in sight, but that was the beauty of hair dye.

"You have some nerve just showing up over here, you know that?" Dina finally said.

"Dina, I don't know what you think happened back then, but it didn't." Diana said, and Dina chortled.

"So, after all these years you still can't admit it."

"Admit what?"

"That you were fucking my husband!"

There it was, the reason why Diana had battled with herself about going over there in the first place. It was something Dina would never be able to let go. It was also the reason why Diana wasn't allowed to see Boogie anymore when he was just a boy. Dina knew Barry and Diana had to do business with each other, but the one thing she could control was who her son was around.

"Are we going to have this conversation again?" Diana sighed.

"We're going to have it until you're woman enough to admit to me that you did it. And then I want an apology."

Diana sighed again and looked up at the ceiling. When she looked back into Dina's awaiting face, she couldn't help but wonder why the thought of something between her and Barry bothered Dina so much, besides the obvious fact that they were married. Early on, Diana sensed that Dina didn't love him the way a wife should love her husband. But then again, that could have just been Diana's distrust of most people. Either way, it was a fact that back in that time, she and Barry had been close friends. She could see how it could easily be perceived as more.

"I'm sorry," Diana started, and she saw Dina sit up straighter. "I'm sorry if you think that something happened between Barry and me. We really were great friends. And I hope now you can let it go."

"You can go straight to hell, Diana," Dina spat out. "I don't know what was worse, that he cheated on me with a woman who disguises the whore in herself through a business, or that our names are so similar. Barry sure did know how to pick them."

"I'm not trying to be respectful in your home, but I would suggest you choose your next words wisely."

"Or what?" Dina challenged. "You might have everyone else around here shaking in their boots, but I'll be the first to tell you that I have never been intimidated by you."

"I guess that's why twenty-odd years later you're still crying about if I slept with your husband," Diana said and instantly regretted it.

"Get the fuck out of my house. Get out!" Dina jumped to her feet and jabbed her finger toward the door.

"Dina, wait." Diana briefly closed her eyes and took a deep breath. "That was very unbecoming of me. Sit down, please. I didn't come to fight. I came to talk about Boogie."

Dina glared down at her before letting her arm drop to her side. Reluctantly, she sat back down on the firm couch and picked up her tea. She sipped it, and Diana gave her a few moments to gather herself.

"What about my son is it that you want to discuss?" she finally asked.

"Do you know what he's been up to?"

"Running his father's businesses better than Barry ever could have. Over and underground."

"I could disagree," Diana said. "But besides that, has he discussed anything else with you?"

"Like the fact that he wants to take majority control over New York? Yes."

"So then you know that we won't just allow that. And you know he's waging war."

"I do. And I guess you're here to what? Get me to talk him out of it, I suppose."

"In the simplest terms, yes."

"Well, I can't do that." Dina shrugged. "Even if I could, why would I?"

"To save your son's life! This is a dangerous game he's playing."

"Or is it a dangerous game you're playing? You wouldn't be here if you weren't worried," Dina said, and Diana didn't like the sly smile that came to her lips.

"No. I wouldn't be here if I didn't truly care about Boogie."

"Care about him? You don't give a damn about my son."

"No, I don't think you give a damn about Boogie. He's going to get hurt, Dina. Or worse, killed."

"You have no idea what my son is capable of, do you?" Dina asked seriously. "My son is the quickest study I have ever met in my life. He adapts so well to change and infiltrates! In just a matter of weeks, he has doubled the profit of every single one of Barry's businesses, and guess what? Now he wants more. There is nothing in this world that can stop a driven force. Stand in his way if you want to, but you will fall. He is prepared to do whatever it takes to see his task through."

The way she said it told Diana that she really believed her own words. The fire behind them also let Diana know she believed that her son would come out on top. The worrisome thing was Dina knew firsthand the power Boogie would be going against, yet she still felt that he would win an all-out war. Something about it all wasn't sitting right.

"Then I guess we have nothing else to talk about," Diana said and stood up.

"I guess we don't. I hope this isn't the last time I see you."

"Right sentence, wrong person. Call your son and repeat it."

With that, Diana left. When the brisk air hit her face, she tried not to look around. Everything reminded her of Barry, and the entire time she was inside of the house, she tried not to let the memories flood her brain. But it was so hard not to, especially since there were so many fond ones. She and Barry had a friendship that nobody but the two of them could understand. She could be her authentic self with him, and for that, she loved him.

It was true when she had said she and Barry were great friends. For a while, that was all it was. They didn't fall in love until much later. He was her favorite person in the world. Not only did he match her in every way, but he made her laugh. Him marrying Dina wasn't the thing that broke her heart. She always blamed herself for it. She could never muster up the courage to tell him her true feelings, and by the time she did, he already had a ring on his finger. Their affair went on until a day in 1994 when he broke her heart.

There was nothing better than feeling the man you love make love to you with his mouth. Diana's hands caressed the back and top of Barry's head as he sucked every drop of juice she had out of her pussy. They'd already made love in the hotel bed twice, but he never could seem to get enough of her. Diana's back arched as her love came down and she felt the last of her energy leave her body. She couldn't take it anymore and pushed him away.

"Baby, what you have is lethal," she said breathlessly. "I can't take it."

"There was once a time where it was me feeling that way about you." Barry grinned when he came up for air.

He kissed her gently on the lips and fell on the bed beside her. He was right; there was once a time where Diana could go all night. But lately, she'd just been too tired. She turned her body so that she could study every inch of his face. He was such a handsome man, and there was nothing she didn't like, from the soft hair on his head to his strong jaw structure and his juicy lips. She reached her hand up and began playing with his goatee.

"I love you, Barry Tolliver."

"I love you too, baby. You know that."

"Mm-hmm, then why isn't it me with the ring on my finger?" she teased.

"That would have never happened had I known you felt the way you do about me."

Diana never thought that she would be in an entanglement with a married man, but there she was, sneaking to hotels every few days just to get some alone time with him. Barry wasn't just anybody, either. He was her colleague. Still, her love for him was so mighty that she wanted to shout it to the mountaintops. She hated that something that felt so right was happening at the wrong time. She was tired of practicing discretion and sneaking around with him like some whore in the night. She wanted him all to herself, and there was something she needed to tell him.

"Barry," she started and paused.

"What, baby?"

"Barry, I . . ." She took a deep breath. *"I want you to leave your wife. I want us to be together for real."*

She didn't know what kind of reaction she would get, but she was hoping for a happy one. What she got was exactly the opposite. The moment the words were out of her mouth, Barry turned over on his back and put his hand over his face for a brief second. When he removed it, he let out a long breath.

"I can't do that, Diana."

"What do you mean you can't do that?" Diana sat up. *"You love me. I know for a fact you love me more than you do her."*

"It's not that easy."

"How isn't it? Just tell her you want a divorce."

"Diana, what's wrong with what we have going on? It works! We both get what we want."

"That's bullshit and you know it. The way I feel about you is a way that I've never felt about any man in my life. I want to be with you. I don't want to keep watching somebody else have you."

"Baby, you know you and I could never really be together. It would be too dangerous."

"We would work it out!"

"Diana, listen—"

"No, Barry. You listen. If you really loved me, you would—"

"She's pregnant."

His words cut like a saw to her chest. She felt her mouth slightly ajar as she tried to sort out her feelings. First she wanted to make sure she heard him correctly.

"She's what?"

"Pregnant, Diana. My wife is pregnant."

"How long have you known?" she asked and watched the guilt spread over his face. *"How long have you known!"*

"About a month."

"A month?" Diana didn't know what was stronger at the moment, her hurt or her shock. *"You've known she was pregnant for a month and you didn't say a word."*

"I know how this must seem, but it wasn't planned. I just didn't know how to tell you."

"How about you say, 'my wife is pregnant' before you shove your dick all up in my pussy? Oh, wait. You knew you wouldn't have gotten any if I knew that!"

Diana hopped up from the bed in a frenzy. Barry tried to grab her arm, but she just snatched away. She began putting her clothes back on and refusing to look at *him, partially because she was so angry, but more so he wouldn't see the tears forming in her eyes.*

He was having a baby with Dina. He was starting a family. She knew there was no way he would get a divorce now. Even if she . . .

"Diana, please don't do this."

Barry came up behind her and wrapped his arms around her. She pushed him off of her and finished buckling her pants. At that point, she didn't care if he saw her cry. She was hurt.

"Do what? Leave you the hell alone?"

"Baby . . ."

"Don't! You don't get to break my heart and comfort me. Pick one! I can't believe you."

"You knew I was married when we first started messing around," Barry said, and Diana wanted to slap the hell out of him.

"And you knew I loved you before we ever even slept together! You knew that! You said we would be together."

"I'm sorry."

"Yeah, I bet you are." Diana snatched up her purse and headed for the door. On the way out, she glanced at her untouched wine glass on the nightstand and turned to him. "You will never have me in this way again."

And he never did. It took her a while to be able to even be his friend again. If business wasn't involved, Barry didn't see her. Boogie was one year old when she finally started coming around Barry casually again. A bond like the one they shared always found its way back. It was hard at first, but the love that she couldn't give to Barry, she gave to Boogie. She grew so attached to him that

Barry named her his godmother. It was a strange turn of events, but she welcomed Boogie into her life for five years, until Dina suspected something was fishy about the relationship Diana had with her husband. The craziest thing was at that point, the romance between them had fizzled out. There was nothing going on, but maybe it was just their chemistry. Losing both Barry and Boogie turned Diana harder than she already was.

She had been angry when she found out about Boogie's conception and now, she might have to be the one to end his life. The irony.

Chapter 7

The Sugar Trap was the place to be every weekend, and as usual, the place was packed to capacity with Harlem's most known faces that Friday night. The streets had been quiet for a week, but that didn't mean anything to Diana. She stayed ready. However, business had to continue, and Friday meant it was time to collect dues.

She sat in her office, surrounded by soundproof walls, wearing a pink blazer dress and a fur draped on her shoulders. In her hand was a pen made of pure gold as she went down a list of names in a black book. She was sitting at her big, black desk checking the names of who all had made their payments and who she had left. There were more than a hundred names in the book, but there were only three left who needed to come and pay.

She checked the clock and saw that it read thirty minutes to midnight. Any payment past Friday would tack on an additional fee, and her people knew that. She sighed and leaned back into her office chair. She hated waiting on people.

Her phone began ringing in her Celine, and she saw that the name on the touch screen said Morgan. Morgan was someone who Diana considered to be a protege. She was not a dancer or a prostitute. Diana liked to think of her as more so in management. She was twenty-four years old, but she was a shark when it came to money and business. Diana had hired her as a bartender three years prior, and Morgan had worked her way up. Now she was in charge of keeping the Sugar Trap running smoothly, especially on the days Diana wasn't there. Morgan kept the girls in check and made sure she told Diana about all of the ins and outs going on in the place.

"Hello?" Diana said when she answered the phone.

"Diana, you need to get down here now."

"What's wrong?" Diana sat up in her chair, hearing the alarm in Morgan's voice.

"It's some niggas down here trying to force their way inside the club. I know you said anybody from Barry's camp isn't welcome here anymore, but they're adamant. I had to stop security from shooting them. There are just too many eyes around."

"You did good. Just keep them right there, and here I come."

Diana disconnected the phone and got up. She knew it would only be a matter of time before Boogie started making noise again. Before she left her office, she made sure that her gun was in her large wallet. She tucked it under her arm and exited.

Standing outside her door on either side were her two personal security guards, holding AK-47 assault rifles. Champ and Harley were Diana's younger cousins. They wouldn't dare let a hair on her head be harmed. Where she moved, they moved. She didn't even have to tell them to follow her for them to do exactly that.

When she resurfaced from the back, patrons on the floor respectfully cleared a path for them to walk through.

She stepped more smoothly than a model on a runway, never giving anyone in particular eye contact. Her attention was on the commotion at the front door. When the four Dominican men Diana had manning the front door saw her approaching, they stepped aside. Morgan was standing in front of four men going off at the mouth. Under any other circumstance, seeing her slim-thick, five-foot-five frame going at it with men that towered over her would have been comical. But it was the fact that Diana knew her rage was coming from a place of feeling deeply disrespected.

"You muthafuckas need to go find some business!" Morgan was snapping.

"We found some, but y'all won't let us be great," the man that stood in front of the others said.

It was Barry's nephew, Tazz. Diana had only known him to be respectful, but then again, that was when Barry was in charge of things. All four men were dressed in street attire and seemed to be harmless, but Diana knew better.

"Tazz, what a surprise. I wish I could say it was a pleasant one." Diana gently moved Morgan to the side and took her place in front of Tazz.

"Yo, Diana, tell these big-body-ass niggas to let us in. We just want to have a good time like everybody else." Tazz pointed at one of the goons.

"I can't do that, and you know I can't," Diana said with a small smile frozen on her lips.

They had a staring standoff until finally, he dropped the harmless act. He chuckled and dropped his arms so that one was on top of the other. He held his head high and his shoulders back as his stare turned into a piercing gaze.

"It was smart of you to tighten up on security," he said evenly. "I'm glad you know that my cousin isn't playin' any games."

"I tightened up on security because your cousin is letting his emotions get the best of him. Now, I assume you came here for a real reason."

"I did."

"Boy, spit it out. You came here all rough and tough. Don't get to acting slow now. You're wasting my time and money."

She could tell that Tazz was annoyed by her words and clenched his jaw. He looked away into space for a moment as if to regain his wits before turning back to her.

"Boogie sent us. I told him we should just make our move on you. Just a clean sweep to get you out of the way."

"I think you should know that bosses never listen to runners," Diana spat. "I assume he told you no and sent you here to talk to me one last time."

"He did. He wants to offer you hood asylum. He said that if you join him and help with his cause, then he would make sure that you remain untouchable."

"He wants me to help him go after my brothers to save my own ass?" Diana chortled. "The nerve of him."

"It's a good deal. You should take it."

"It's obvious Boogie doesn't really have the force to go against us. That's why he needs me. My answer is now and forever no."

"I don't think you're recognizing Boogie's grace in his offer," Tazz told her and shook his head. "He could care less about the other two, but you? For some reason, he has a soft spot for you. This offer has nothin' to do with his ability to wipe you all out."

"Is that right?"

"It's right. You may look twenty years younger than what you are, but deep inside you know that you don't have what it takes to lose this war, old lady."

Diana felt her left eye twitch. Tazz had indeed struck a nerve. In Diana's mind, she felt like she could live forever, but physics said otherwise. Although she was healthy as an ox for her age, she knew that she was weaker than she once had been. There was a time when she would fight in the field with her soldiers, but now she just gave the orders, and they fulfilled her requests. However, to have someone who only existed because of what she, Barry, Marco, Li, and Caesar had built from the ground up disrespecting her lit a fire in her belly.

Her body moved before her mind even gave it the okay. In a swift motion, she chopped Tazz in the neck, making him stumble back. She placed a foot behind his ankle and jerked it, tripping him. As he was falling back, Diana removed the Beretta from her purse and cocked it. By the time Tazz realized what had happened, he was on his ass and staring up into the barrel of her gun. Her goons drew their weapons as well and put them on the rest of Boogie's men.

"I'm going to give you two seconds to get the fuck off my property before your fucking head is nothing but noodles. You tell Boogie I said over my dead body."

"I'm sure he can make that happen," Tazz sneered and got to his feet. He motioned for the other men to follow him. "Let's go."

Diana watched them walk away into the night. She forgot all about the people that she was waiting on to pay their dues. They probably had shown up to her office and she wasn't there. But right then, she didn't care. She didn't remember the last time someone had sent disrespect at her the way Boogie had. But then again, calm could only last for so long. She turned to Morgan, who was looking at her with wide eyes.

"I–I've never seen anything like that. You just dropped a grown-ass man."

"Well, get used to it," Diana said absentmindedly before she looked at Champ.

"Ma'am?"

"I need around-the-clock protection on my businesses and my girls until further notice."

"You said it, so it will be done."

He stepped away and pulled out a burner flip phone. Diana's adrenaline rushed as she put her gun away. She knew she wouldn't be able to just sit back while others did her bidding. Boogie had made it personal.

"Morgan, I want you to go home right now," Diana said before she went back inside the building.

"But the night just started. I have to make sure the girls working tonight are okay. I know you saw Tony's drunk ass is there. He always fucks with Baby Girl, and I'm scared he's gonna drug her if I don't watch his ass."

"Morgan." Diana pushed the girls loose, long curls out of her face to look into her brown eyes. "Go home. I'll be sure to have your house covered."

"I'm not leaving you," Morgan said, still defying her words. "Not after something like that just happened."

"I don't think you understand the seriousness behind all of this."

"I don't need to understand anything to know I'm not leaving you alone."

"Your loyalty will be your undoing one day."

"Then you should have never hired me."

Diana recognized the fire in Morgan's eyes. She had the same fire when she was her age. It was bred from the embers of fearlessness. Eventually, Diana just gave in. She nodded and motioned for Morgan to come back into the building. The two of them went and sat at the bar together, with Champ and Harley standing not too far away. Diana called for the bartender to pour them the house special.

The music was blasting, and the strobe lights set the tone in the dark club. One of the Sugar Trap's most popular girls, Denim, had taken the stage. Diana watched her climb all the way to the top of the pole and drop into the splits. The crowd went crazy, and every man close to the stage threw handfuls of money her way. That was good, because Denim was one of the girls who still owed her dues. Now Diana knew she would have no reason not to pay up.

She turned her attention to Morgan, who was sipping on the Long Island iced tea the bartender had just placed in front of her.

"What I want to know is what were you going to do up against those big-ass men?" Diana asked, trying to hide her smirk.

"What do you mean what was I gonna do?" Morgan asked and pulled a switchblade from her YSL crossbody.

"I was going to stab the closest motherfucka to me in the throat and hope the niggas behind me lit the rest up before they got to me!"

Diana laughed at the visual. She didn't know Morgan had so much fire in her. It was a good thing to have, but dangerous.

"You're entirely too pretty to be getting blood on your hands," Diana told her, which was the truth. Morgan had fair skin and a face as pretty as a Barbie. She was obviously mixed, but her hair had just enough kink in it to show her black roots.

"I'm sure they said the same about you when you were my age."

"They did," Diana admitted. "But the difference between you and I is that I was born into this. You come from a good home."

"Yeah, so good that I didn't go to college and I work at a gentleman's club."

"Hey." Diana raised her eyebrow. "Don't forget that I pay you the salary of a CEO."

"This is true. Cheers to that!" Morgan laughed and held up her glass.

Diana picked hers up and clanked it against Morgan's. She drank a large gulp, welcoming the buzz that would inevitably come. She needed it.

"Morgan, do you have a gun?" she asked randomly.

"Yes."

"Start carrying it on you every day. Even when you aren't at work, okay?"

"Okayyy," Morgan said curiously. "Does this have anything to do with what just happened outside?"

"Yes," Diana answered truthfully.

The only people in her fold that knew about Boogie's proposed threat were her shooters. Everyone else, including her girls and Morgan, had been left out of the loop. She didn't want to cause alarm in her camp, not without first trying to eradicate the threat.

"What's going on?" Morgan asked.

"Nothing you need to worry yourself with. Just stay protected, okay?"

"All right."

"When Denim is done with her dance, send her to my office," Diana said before she downed the rest of her drink.

"Man, how come you ain't tell me that Diana got down like that?" Tazz sat in the backseat of Boogie's Dodge Ram, rubbing his neck.

Boogie had been waiting around the corner from the Sugar Trap for him with Bentley. The other men that were with Tazz went on about their business, but the three of them had one more stop to make, one Boogie didn't trust anyone else to make. He laughed as Tazz recanted what had just happened, and he couldn't get the painted image of Diana dropping him like it was nothing out of his head.

"It's a reason she is who she is and why she has so much respect in these streets," Boogie told him when he was done laughing.

"Yeah, a'ight. I should have dropped her old ass, but I don't hit women."

"Diana isn't just a woman. She's a boss," Boogie said absentmindedly.

"You're speakin' mighty high about someone who you just threatened," Bentley pointed out.

"I'm just speakin' facts," Boogie responded. "My pops always spoke highly of her. He also taught me never to underestimate my enemy."

Tazz's biggest mistake was assuming that just because Diana was an older woman, she was weak. Boogie knew she wasn't, which was why he had tried one last attempt to get her to join him. Deep inside, he knew she wouldn't. Not yet. Eventually, they all would come around to seeing things his way. He would just have to force their hands.

"I guess Tazz learned that shit the hard way," Bentley said with a chuckle.

"Yeah, ha ha. Laugh it up, nigga."

Boogie listened to them go back and forth the rest of the drive from Diana's place to Chinatown. It was colorful and, as usual, lit up in the nighttime. It was known that Li did his business in the basement of a Chinese restaurant called Fortune and usually arrived around midnight.

"There he go," Bentley noted and pointed.

Sure enough, Li was stepping out of a Maserati. He was taller than most Chinese men Boogie had seen in his life, and for an older gentleman, he still had a muscular build. The hair on the top of his head had gray sprinkled all throughout it, and he wore a blue two-button suit.

Li held his arm out, and a beautiful woman in a red sequined dress stepped out of the car with him. She was black and petite with a pretty face. If Boogie wasn't mistaken, she was one of Diana's girls. The two of them were instantly surrounded by bodyguards. It pleased Boogie to see them taking his threat so seriously. However, the only bad thing about bodyguards was that they bled and died too.

"Y'all ready?" Boogie asked.

"Hell yeah," Tazz said.

"Yup."

"Make the call," Boogie instructed, and Bentley pulled out a flip phone.

"Y'all in position?" Bentley asked when the person on the other end answered. He paused for a split second before speaking again. "'A'ight, wait for the signal."

"Let's get it," Boogie said when Bentley disconnected the call.

The three men slid ski masks over their faces, and Bentley and Tazz pulled out their guns. Boogie slowed the truck in front of the building that Li was making his way to and rolled down the windows on the passenger side. When he was at a full-blown stop, he took a breath and began to yell out of the window.

"Li!" he called. "Boogie sends his love!"

Li's bodyguards tried to brandish their weapons, but they were too slow. Bentley and Tazz let their guns do their talking, and their bullets hit all of their targets. Blood splattered all over the concrete, and bodies dropped left and right as the automatic weapons rang out. It was mayhem, and the innocent bystanders on the sidewalk were running in shrieks of terror. One of their bullets had hit the woman Li was with, and he was using her dead body as a shield.

When it was only him left, Boogie motioned for Bentley and Tazz to stop shooting. Li was all alone, with no hired hands to protect him. He wanted Li to feel helpless, like there wasn't any place safe in the world for him to hide from Boogie, because there wasn't, and now he knew that he wasn't untouchable. Boogie wanted him to feel exactly how his father had felt when he was tortured to death.

Removing the mask from his face, Boogie saw the uneasy expression on Li's.

"Oops, my bad. I meant *I* send my love," Boogie shouted.

He drove off quickly and left Li to tend to his dead men. There was no way better to do a job than to do it yourself to make sure it got done correctly. He could have easily waited for Shamar's shooters to handle his light weight, but Boogie needed people to know that he wasn't afraid to make moves himself, and after that night, they would.

He'd made the call to Shamar and accepted his offer a few days prior, which Shamar honored by sending his shooters ahead of his own arrival the following day. Boogie wasn't stupid. He knew Shamar had his own agenda. Boogie planned to watch him closely. However, in the meantime, all that mattered was that they were on the same page.

Knowing he would have the extra manpower was what made Boogie attack the Chinese first. The explosion at Marco's factory was nothing in comparison to what he had just done. He figured the Chinese would want to get revenge, but they would be too busy planning a funeral.

He nodded at Bentley when they were far enough away from the restaurant. Bentley pulled the flip phone back out and redialed the same number.

"Is he inside?" Bentley asked and waited for an answer. "Then do it."

Bentley put the phone on speaker, and Boogie listened to the loud explosion of the bombs his men had put inside of Fortune. It was the sweet sound of another piece getting knocked off the board.

Chapter 8

Diana was buried deep under her covers when the back-to-back ringing of her phone woke her up. She'd tried to ignore it, especially since it had taken so long to fall asleep in the first place, but whoever was phoning her was relentless. She grumbled to herself when she looked at the digital clock on her nightstand and saw that it was three in the morning. Her attitude changed, however, when she saw that it was Marco trying to get in touch with her. He'd called her eight times, and Marco was the type who never called more than once. She dialed him back, and he answered on the first ring.

"Diana?"

"It's me. Is everything all right?" she asked, and her mind instantly went to Caesar. "Did something happen to Caesar?"

"No, it's . . ."

"It's what?" she asked, hearing the hesitant tone in his voice.

"It's Li."

"What about Li?"

"He was killed tonight."

It took her a while to process his words. She had to sit up in bed and rub her eyes with her fingers to make sure she was awake. Had she heard him correctly?

"Killed as in dead?" she asked.

"That's the only way you can be after somebody killed you."

"Was it Boogie?"

"We think so. His place was hit with the same kind of explosives mine was. It looks pretty bad."

"You're still there?" Diana said, getting up from her bed. "I'm on my way."

"Nah, you stay where you're at," Marco told her. "As a matter of fact, if it was this easy for him to get to Li, maybe you should get out of your house. Go and stay somewhere else for a while."

"All right," she said.

"And Diana?"

"Yeah?"

"I know you didn't want to kill him, but I don't think we have a choice now. It's him or us."

Diana didn't say anything, and Marco disconnected the phone. She didn't want to admit it out loud, but he was right. Boogie had proven himself to be a force to be reckoned with. He killed Li in his own place of business. That was something Caesar wouldn't have done. Boogie must have done it after he'd sent his cousin to intimidate her, and Diana couldn't help but to wonder if he had retaliated because she had told him no.

Before she fell back into her bed, something told Diana to check the security footage on her phone. The first thing that caught her eye was that she didn't see any of her shooters guarding the doors to her home. Suddenly, she heard a noise outside her bedroom door. Instinct kicked in, and she grabbed the .22 she kept in the night-stand beside her bed. She walked quietly to the bedroom door in her wine-colored silk nightgown and counted to three before she opened the door and aimed her gun.

"Don't shoot!" A nervous voice sounded, and Diana sighed in relief when Morgan stepped from the shadows.

"Girl, I could have killed you!" Diana exclaimed.

Diana had closed the club early that night and made Morgan come home with her. She was glad that she did, because who knew what could have happened?

Morgan stood there, looking wide-eyed in a short yellow pajama set. Her hair was tucked under her bonnet, and she had a pair of Diana's Gucci slippers on her feet.

"I thought I heard something," she said and looked at the gun in Diana's hand. "You must have heard it too."

"No, I heard you. But there's nobody standing guard out front or back," Diana said in a low tone and tried to listen to her house. "Under the mattress of the bed in the guest room you're in is a pistol. Grab it and follow me."

Morgan didn't ask any questions. She just did what she was told and met Diana back at the entrance of her room. Diana showed her how to take it off safety and cock it back. She didn't know why, but she just had an eerie feeling looming over her. Her men never left their posts, even if they had to pee. Something was going on.

Morgan crept closely behind Diana as they quietly bounded down the spiral staircase. The house was dark, but there were nightlights all around that illuminated their way.

"You check the back," Diana whispered when they got to the main level of the home. "If you see anyone, shoot them."

"Okay," Morgan whispered back.

When she was gone, Diana checked her surroundings. She didn't hear anything out of the ordinary, nor did she see anything out of place. The only way someone would have gotten in her house undetected was if they knew the security code. But even if they did, the sound of her alarm going off would have woken her up long before Marco's phone call. Nevertheless, something was amiss.

Aiming her gun, she inched toward the front door, feeling the cold marble floors under her bare feet with each step. Her breathing became shallow, and she knelt down just in case she had to shoot from an angle. Wrapping a hand around the level handle, she turned it slowly and snatched open the door.

She'd braced herself, but when Diana was met with nothing but cold air, she stood up and stepped on the porch. There were no cars in her driveway, but she did notice that the entrance to the gate surrounding her home was open. Someone had been there. Her eyes fell on some red streaks on the concrete that led all the way to her precious rose bush in front of her home. Her common sense was telling her to go back inside and call somebody, but the curiosity in her won the battle. She walked beside the fresh blood and braced herself to see her men lying dead in her roses. What she saw, however, was much worse.

"Buttercup," Diana breathed.

Sprawled in a sickishly twisted angle was one of Diana's best girls. Unlike others that had to be punished, Buttercup had never stepped out of line. She'd worked her way up from the Sugar Trap a few years ago and had been a high-paid escort ever since. Due to the small commotion at the Sugar Trap, Diana had forgotten that Li booked Buttercup that night. She was his favorite and always paid extra for her time. Buttercup must have gotten shot outside of the restaurant, because there were bullet holes in her pretty red dress. Poking out from her cleavage was a folded piece of paper.

Diana grabbed it. When she unfolded it, she read the question written in sloppy handwriting out loud. "*What about now*?" Diana balled up the piece of paper and threw it down on Buttercup's body.

"Diana, all of your people are dead and piled up by the fire pit in the back!" Morgan's voice sounded as she appeared at Diana's side. When Diana didn't react or say anything, she looked down to see what her eyes were transfixed on. "Is that . . . Is that Buttercup?"

"Yes."

"Who would do something like this?"

"Bryshon Tolliver. Li was murdered tonight too."

"But why?"

"Men do merciless things when they don't know where to direct their anger. He thinks he wants to be king of New York, but really he just wants his father back," Diana said sadly. "And since that can't happen, we all are going to suffer."

"He killed one of your girls. What are you gonna do?"

"The correct question isn't what am I going to do. The right one to ask is why haven't I done anything yet."

"Why haven't you?"

"The same reason why he keeps trying to get me to join him. We don't want to hurt each other."

"But why? He clearly doesn't give a damn. Look at Buttercup!"

"I don't think he meant to kill her. I think this was just a case of the wrong place, wrong time."

"Why are you defending him?" Morgan asked. "There's a massacre in the back yard."

Diana looked into Morgan's eyes and wished that she could find the words to explain, but she couldn't.

"Grab your things. We can't stay here," was all she said as she headed back inside.

She would call someone to clean up the mess at her home. Diana was glad that she didn't have neighbors. It made things like that easier to cover up. She didn't bother to stop and take a look at the gruesome scene in her backyard. She just walked up the stairs to her room and let her memory take control of her.

"Godmommy, these are for you!"

A much younger Diana turned around from the flowers she was planting to see a handsome young boy with missing front teeth holding some dandelions in his hand. The dirt dangling from the roots were how she knew that they were freshly ripped from the earth. She smiled and took them, kissing the boy gently on the forehead.

"Oh, Boogie, they're beautiful! How did you know yellow was my favorite color?"

"I thought blue was your favorite?"

"Well, now yellow is. Just for you," she said and tickled him.

He laughed uncontrollably, and they both fell into the grass. She snuggled him close and gave him another kiss on the head. As he did most Sundays since he'd turned one year old, Boogie found himself at Diana's house.

During his wife's pregnancy, Barry and Diana barely spoke, not even at the monthly meetings each family head had to attend. That was why, shortly after Boogie's first birthday, she was shocked when Barry came to visit her with the baby in tow. Diana wanted to hate Boogie; she really did. He was the reason why her happily-ever-after didn't happen. But one look into his cute, innocent face, she realized she couldn't. A love she had only felt once in her life welled up in her chest at the first sight of him. So when Barry asked her to be his godmother, she said yes. She knew Barry was using that as a reason to have some sort of relationship with her, and she was okay with that.

"Why are you always planting flowers, Godmommy?" Boogie asked, looking up at her.

"Planting flowers teaches patience," she said. "It reminds me that if I work for it and be patient, there will be a beautiful outcome."

"Beautiful like you."

"Thank you, my baby. Are you hungry?" she asked even though she knew the answer. That boy could eat!

"Yeah! Can you make me some pork chops?"

"Boy, it's lunchtime. How about a sandwich and some chips? I'll even let you drink a big glass of juice."

"Yay!"

"All right, let's hurry before your father gets here."

Hand in hand, the two of them headed into the house. The kitchen was right by the back yard, so the patio had the prettiest view. She sat him at the table and let the sunrays shine on his smooth brown skin. Just as she went to start making him her famous PB&J, the doorbell sounded.

"Daddy!" Boogie exclaimed with his arms up.

She checked the clock on the stove and saw that it was only just after noon. Barry usually didn't come get him until around two. She figured maybe he wanted to get him early, which was fine, but he should have called.

When she got to the front door, she didn't look into the peephole to see who it was. The guard at her gate wouldn't have let anyone up that she didn't know.

"You're right on time! I was just about to make lunch—Oh!" Diana stopped talking when she saw that it was not Barry at her door.

"Where is my son?" Dina Tolliver asked tersely. Dina stood there wearing heels, a pink skirt suit, and a white clutch tucked tightly under her arm. Her hair was freshly done, as were her nails. She looked like the perfect trophy wife.

Diana was completely caught off guard, and she looked behind Dina to see if Barry was in the car. He wasn't. Diana gathered herself and looked back at Dina and could see that she wasn't in the best of moods. She rarely came to Diana's house. Most times Barry dropped Boogie off, he was alone.

"He's in the kitchen. I was about to make him a sandwich."

"That won't be necessary, now or ever," Dina said and stepped past Diana and started down the wide hallway. *"Boogie! Get your things. It's time to go."*

"Is something wrong?" Diana asked, trying to place Dina's behavior.

"Yes, actually something is very wrong." Dina whipped around to face her. *"You and Barry."*

"What about me and Barry?"

Dina scoffed and opened her clutch. From it, she pulled a piece of paper and handed it to Diana. It was a hotel receipt from five years ago.

"Valentine's Day," Dina said as Diana continued to stare at the paper. *"That's a hotel receipt from Valentine's Day. I found it in Barry's sock drawer, and I can tell you something. He's never taken me to a hotel room on Valentine's Day. Turn it over."*

Diana didn't need to. She knew what was on the back. But to save face, she did. Written in cursive were the words I love you. *It was her handwriting, because of course she had written it. It was how she'd first told him she loved him. At the time, she couldn't say it out loud, so she wrote it down and snuck it in his pants pocket to find later on. What was shocking to her was that he'd held on to it for all those years.*

"I don't know what I'm supposed to do with this," Diana said and handed Dina back the receipt. "What does a receipt found in your husband's drawer have to do with me?"

"Oh, please stop the charade! I always thought the two of you had something going on. I bet if I were to find something with your handwriting on it, it would match up with what's on the back of that receipt. Boogie! I said let's go!"

Dina turned and continued down the hallway toward the kitchen.

"Dina, wait—"

"It's one thing to sleep with another woman's husband, but the fact that he made you the godmother of my child. Ha! You will never see my son again."

"Dina, there's nothing going on between me and Barry," Diana said, which was the truth. She and Barry hadn't slept together in years. "Please don't bring Boogie into this. Don't take him from me."

Dina ignored her. Instead, she went and snatched a confused Boogie from his seat and nearly dragged him back to the front door.

"Wait! Godmommy was about to make me a sandwich."

"Don't you ever call her that again!" Dina said and pointed a finger in his scared face. "Do you understand me? You're not coming over here anymore!"

*Her words were cutting Diana deeper than any knife
ever could. She watched helplessly as Boogie reached
for her, but she couldn't do anything. Boogie somehow
wrestled out of Dina's grip and ran into Diana's arms.*

*"Godmommy, you don't want to see me anymore?" he
asked tearfully.*

*"Oh, honey, of course I do," Diana said, wiping the
drops of water from his eyes. "Your mommy just said
you have to go. But listen to me. No matter what, always
remember that I love you. Okay? No matter how big you
get or how far you go, I will always love you."*

*"I love you too," Boogie said right before Dina
snatched him away again.*

*He reached for her all the way up until he was in the
car. Even when he was there, he looked longingly back at
the house. Diana stood at the front door with her hand
on her chest. She was trying as hard as she could to bite
back her tears.*

*Before getting into the car, Dina looked back up at
Diana. "I meant what I said. Stay the hell away from my
son. He will forget you. I'm going to make sure of that."*

Diana came back to reality and shook the memory of
Dina driving off with Boogie out of her head. For years,
Diana thought that Dina had made good on her word to
make Boogie forget her. But now she wasn't so sure.

Chapter 9

A muffled scream danced on both of Shamar's ear-drums. It was like music, and the corners of his mouth twitched, itching to smile. He loved the sound of deep regret that came with crossing him, because he was more than a menace; he was a monster. He was sure that Daryl Jenkins, one of his long-time dope boys, regretted selling all the coke Shamar had trusted him with and using the money to try to skip town.

It wasn't the missing money that bothered Shamar. It was the principle behind it.

Daryl was a dark-skinned man in his early thirties who had been working for Shamar since before he was twenty-one. Although he was still had a young-looking face, his receding hairline and thinning top betrayed him. His actions had come as a shock to Shamar. Daryl knew better, but still he didn't do better. Now, there he was tied up on the ground in a pained fetal position and bleeding from his nose.

They were in an old outdoor car wash on the outskirts of town. It would be easy to clean up any mess after Shamar was done with him. Two of Shamar's young goons were having at him in the worst way, while Shamar's highest ranked street general, Frost, stood next to him. Frost could have been considered Shamar's right-hand man if he believed in friendship, but Shamar didn't consider anyone a friend. Daryl's actions had proved that anybody would bite the hand that fed them if a new purpose suited them, so Frost was more of an ally that Shamar could trust. Frost had never done anything to make Shamar make him question where his loyalty lay, which was why he was there standing beside him.

"I guess even loyalty has an expiration date," Shamar said when his boys finally let Daryl breathe.

He looked up at Shamar from the ground with only one eye. The other was swollen shut and had a bloody gash under it. Still, he had a look of defiance that made Shamar think he hadn't been beaten long enough. Daryl breathed hard and heavily. It was apparent that he was angry, which led Shamar to believe that his screams behind the duct tape covering his mouth weren't from regret at all. He snatched the tape away, and Daryl flinched from the sting.

"You tried to run off on me, Daryl," Shamar said and made the "tsk-tsk" sound with his tongue. "Do you have any idea of what happens to men who cross me?"

"Yeah," Daryl said in between breaths. "The same thing that happened to your son. Except the niggas that did that are still alive."

His words made Shamar hold his inhaled breath for a second longer. Daryl was bold to ever speak on Shane, but he was even bolder to weaponize his words. Shamar backhanded him with his fist. Daryl grunted but turned his good eye on Shamar again with the same glare.

"You ain't been hearing what they're saying about you?"

"Enlighten me," Shamar said and knelt down so that he was at eye level with Daryl.

"That you're weak. You ordered us to go and help defend the same people that killed your son. A lot of us didn't take well to that, and we know it's a matter of time before everyone else sees you for what you really are."

"And what's that?"

"Somebody else's bitch!" Daryl spat out.

Shamar looked at him. He was so close to death, and he knew it. He probably felt so good saying those last words. It probably felt really gangster. But now, it was Shamar's turn to speak.

"One, my son got himself killed by being careless and forgetting the teachings of a boss. That is the price you pay when you move stupidly in the streets. Nobody can save you from yourself. Two, the wisest man knows to always keep his enemies close. It puts you in the best position to strike. And three, thank you for letting me know that there are other snakes in the fold." Shamar stood up and put his hands in the pocket of his coat before turning away.

Before he left the stall, he turned to his young goons and eyed them down. "I want the names of every snake in my camp."

"Got it," one of them said.

Shamar and Frost exited the stall with the sounds of loud thuds and grunts in their wake. They'd ridden in Frost's black armored Tahoe, and as they drove off, Shamar stared out of the darkly tinted windows.

"When my youngins are done with him, I don't want his family to have to mourn him. Put them in body boxes too."

The sinister request was made so casually and without feeling. That was because there *was* no feeling behind it. Shamar wanted to send out a message, as a reminder to anyone who felt that he had gone soft: he was darker than ever before.

"No doubt. It will be handled," Frost said as he drove. "But Daryl, though? I would have never seen that one coming. He tried to run off with two hundred thou! Just stupid."

"All these young niggas are stupid," Shamar told him flatly, still looking out of the window. "They're too busy chasing the bag, no matter the cost, and not taking care of it. If either one isn't done right, you end up fucked up. That's what I used to try and teach my son. He didn't listen either."

"Shane always moved to his own beat, though. But still, the end goal was to always make you proud."

"Well, he never did." Shamar's tone was bitter.

Most couldn't understand the level of disdain Shamar had for his son. They felt that because Shane had been his flesh and blood, he should have felt a deeper loss at his death. But the truth was, the saddest part about Shane's death was the funeral, and that was only because Shamar had to see his ex-wife. The streets saw Shamar doing business with his son's killer as weakness, but in fact it proved just how ruthless of a man he really was. Shamar was as cunning as a snake, and his bite would be just as venomous. The chess game had just begun.

"Well, you know my motto. The show must go on," Frost told him. "And speaking of the show, Monte called me while we were back there. He said they just touched down in New York."

"Good. I'll be there in the morning."

"I'm coming with you."

"No, I need you here in Ohio to make sure everything is in order. You'll be in New York soon enough."

Just like Shamar knew he would, Boogie had called him a few days prior to accept his offer. The call came a little later than expected, but it came nonetheless. The complete details of their arrangement said that once Boogie controlled all of the boroughs, then Shamar would be allotted access to push his work in and out of Manhattan. It was a good deal, but Shamar was a greedy man. Why take a slice when the whole pie was right in front of your face?

"All right. You sure this nigga Boogie is as green as you say?"

"He's so oblivious to everything," Shamar answered. "His judgments are so clouded by his rage that he doesn't realize that the fuel to it is going to be his undoing."

He grew silent and just let his words float in the air around them.

Frost drove Shamar all the way home to his four-story, six-bedroom, seven-bathroom mansion and drove up the long driveway.

"My jet leaves at ten in the morning," Shamar said before getting out of the car.

"I'll be here at eight thirty."

Shamar nodded and stepped down from the vehicle. He walked to the front door of the house, which was being manned by two of his best soldiers. Not many people knew where Shamar stayed, but you couldn't be too careful. He kept security all around his home and even had a few trained pit bulls running around. If anybody showed up there that wasn't supposed to be there, they would be ready to rip their heads off.

"Welcome home, boss," one of the guards said and opened the door.

Shamar acknowledged them with a nod and went through the threshold. Instantly, he was met by his housekeeper, Vetty. She was an elderly woman from Texas and had brought her Southern comfort to Shamar's home. He told her that she could dress casually while she worked, but she still always wore an apron over her shirt and pants. She took his coat from him and dropped his favorite house slippers at his feet. When he removed the Bally loafers from his feet, she took them and placed them in the hallway closet near the front door.

"Take them to my room, Vetty," Shamar told her, confused because that's what she always did.

"I would, but *she* told me I wasn't allowed to come in there right now."

"She?" Shamar inquired. "You let someone in my room while I was gone?"

"She made it past security." Vetty shrugged her shoulders. "I figured it was out of my hands, sugar. Dinner will be done in a few hours."

On that note, Vetty took her leave. Shamar loosened his tie and headed for the staircase to see who had been let in his house. The only person he could think of was his ex-wife, Camella, and if it were her, he prepared himself to shoot her where she stood. He couldn't think of a reason why she would be there, though, because she hated him as much as he hated her. Still, she had once lived in the home with him and could possibly have gotten clearance.

He didn't hesitate to swing the master bedroom door open and was startled to see not Camella, but Dina Tolliver, laying in his bed. She was wrapped up in Shamar's thick Versace robe, sipping a tall glass of wine while eating from a plate of chocolate strawberries.

He stared at her silently before going to the bathroom attached to his bedroom to wash Daryl's blood from his hands. When he came back into the room, he removed his tie and unbuttoned his shirt.

Dina wasn't paying him any attention. It was almost as if *he* were a guest in his own home. He tossed his tie over the plate of strawberries to get her attention, and that did it.

"How rude," Dina said, scrunching up her face. "There's no telling what kind of business you handled today."

"I thought we agreed that you weren't going to come until next week," Shamar said.

"Obviously, I didn't want to wait," Dina told him, setting the glass of wine down next to the bed.

In the beginning, Shamar had only known Dina through her husband's right-hand man, Julius. She and Julius never elaborated on their relationship at the time, but it was obvious to Shamar what it was. She loved him. Whether or not he loved her back was up in the air. Julius reminded Shamar of a younger version of himself, a man that would do whatever it took to get on top. The only difference was that Julius was dead, and Shamar was not.

The key to everything had been Dina, so when she called him shortly after Bosco, Caesar, and Julius had died, he jumped at the chance to keep the original plan in motion—with a few changes, of course. At first Shamar didn't know how they were going to pull it all off with Boogie lurking.

"You leave my son to me. All I have to do is keep feeding his anger and he'll bring everything we want to the table. He just doesn't know that he isn't invited to the feast," she'd said.

The business relationship Shamar had with her was going off without a hitch. It was the other part that slightly worried him. Dina was a very alluring woman. For her age, she was stunning, and her body rivaled that of a woman two times younger than her. Shamar was a man about his business, but with Dina, it was easy to fall into her trap because she *was* his business. It happened so fast, and soon he was entangled in her spider web of love.

Standing up from the bed, she walked over to him and kissed him passionately on the lips. Shamar couldn't fight her enchanting ways. He plunged his tongue deeply inside of her mouth. When she pulled her lips back, Shamar still felt the remnants of the kiss on his lips.

She was playing a dangerous game—they both were—and Shamar knew it. He couldn't lie; he'd missed the feel of her soft skin on his. Her sex was some of the best he'd had in years, and that was part of the reason why he wished he'd never dabbled in it to begin with. Now he wanted it all the time.

She let the robe fall from her shoulders and revealed that she was completely naked.

"I've missed you and *this*." She grabbed his already erect penis and lowered her eyes at him.

"You couldn't wait until I was in New York tomorrow?" he asked.

"You know us seeing each other like this is too risky with Boogie sniffing his nose around. And I don't like quickies."

"I know you don't," Shamar said, remembering the hours they'd spent sexing. He gripped the back of her neck and pulled her in for another kiss before coming up for air again. "What are we doing?"

"Enjoying each other," she breathed. "Is that so wrong?"

"Yes, because I'm still trying to figure out if I should trust you or not." Shamar looked down into her eyes, wishing he could see what was behind them.

"I'm the one who reopened the door when Caesar closed it. I want to see you get everything that you desire."

"But what's really in it for you?"

"Being the woman by your side," she said, but he wasn't buying it.

"Don't lie to me," he warned. "You played a part in your husband's death and were willing to kill your own son to be with another man. I know I'm nothing to you. So tell me, what's really in it for you?"

He saw a flicker in her eyes and watched her jaw clench for a split second. Shamar wanted her to know that she couldn't play her normal game with him. He still had a mind outside of his dick, and it worked very well. He might not have known her true motive, but he knew there was one.

"The truth is that I want to start life anew," she said with a sigh. "And before any of the things I've done come back to haunt me, I want to get rid of all the power players and put someone in power who would grant me asylum."

"And how do you know I won't just kill you when I'm done with you?"

"I don't. But then again, you don't know if I'll betray you either. Russian Roulette is funny that way. I guess we'll both find out in the end if the gun is loaded or not," she said breathily and then placed her mouth by his ear. "But for now, I just want you to fuck me."

Her tongue made circular motions on his neck that made the bulge in his slacks even harder. She slid her cool hands on his chest and pinched his nipples. A moan slipped from Shamar's lips, and he stood still and let her have her way with him. When finally she dropped to her knees and pulled his pants down, his third eye had precum drizzling from it. She licked it off like the juice on a melting popsicle. He'd gotten oral from many younger women, but none beat that of a seasoned woman. Dina's gag reflex was nonexistent, and she proved it again when she brought the tip of his dick to the way back of her mouth with no problem.

"Shit," he said, trying to hold his ground. It was hard with the tingly feeling shooting throughout his body. As she worked her magic, a floating sensation came over him. He closed his eyes and couldn't help but to think how much of a shame it was going to be when he had to get rid of her after she helped him take down her son.

They pulled from reality and sexed the night away. Shamar fell asleep feeling the best he had in a while.

When he woke up the next morning, Dina was gone. He reached over to where she had been lying and felt that the bed was still warm there. Getting out of bed, Shamar went to the bathroom so he could shower before his flight. When he finished and was fully dressed, he grabbed his already packed luggage from the closet and left the house. As promised, Frost was already outside and ready to go.

"It feels like a morning for champs," Shamar said after he and his bags were in the car.

Frost took notice of the chipper tone in his voice and raised a brow. Shamar had never been a morning person, especially before a flight. The truth was that Shamar knew that day was the start of something beautiful for him.

"You okay over there?" Frost asked, glancing over at him again.

"Never better," Shamar answered. "I just feel like a man who's walking into a treasure while the keeper is holding the door open for me. I give it a few weeks before my product is the only one pushed through New York. I think I may begin looking at properties this week."

"You sure you ain't moving too fast with it?"

"Swift is the only way to do it. My bite is going to be so quick that Boogie won't even know he's dying slowly until it's too late. He still thinks the only reason I'm coming is to help him get in position, when really I'm boxing him in."

"Your connects still good down there?" Frost asked.

"Yeah," Shamar said and let his thoughts float to Dina. "One of them for sure. The other, I'm meeting later today after I meet with Boogie."

"Be sure to keep me in the loop. Let me know if you need me."

"I'm sure everything will be fine. I sent Bill, Major, and Rocko down there already. They'll be at the airport waiting for me."

Frost dropped Shamar off at a runway where a private jet was waiting for him. Once aboard, Shane got comfortable and took a shot of whiskey before takeoff. He was the only passenger on the luxurious aircraft, but he didn't mind it. He removed his wireless headphones from his Louis Vuitton duffle, put them in his ears, and turned on classical music. It was something that calmed his nerves while he was in the air. Something about a violin playing smoothly eased his mind.

The flight was a quick and smooth, which he was thankful for. Shamar hated when his life was in someone else's hands. It made him feel helpless.

He exited the jet, and parked on the runway was a sleek chocolate brown Rolls Royce. Standing outside of it were Major, Rocko, and Bill. A person might have thought they were modeling for *GQ* magazine in their fur coats and shades. Major was the only one who rocked his long locs down and over his shoulders, while the other two had theirs up in buns. Rocko and Bill grabbed Shamar's bags and loaded them in the car while Major held the back door open for him.

"He just sent us the location of the spot we're supposed to meet him at," Major said.

"Good."

Shamar knew he was speaking of Boogie. He was ready to get the show on the road. He had a very long day ahead of him.

The other two got back in the car, with Bill sitting in the back with him, and they left the landing site. As they drove, Shamar took the time to admire the scenery. New York was a busy place, but it was beautiful and diverse. The perfect place to set up shop.

"We're here," Major announced after almost forty minutes of drive time.

They'd pulled into a truck stop, where a semi-truck and a Lamborghini were parked. When the Rolls Royce slowed to a stop, three men hopped out of the Lamborghini with Mac-10s drawn. When Boogie got out of the driver seat and leaned on his vehicle, Shamar wished he could shoot the smug look off his face.

"What you wanna do, boss?" Major said, eyeing Boogie's goons from the front seat.

"Let's just play their game," Shamar told him, and he nodded.

The three of them got out first, and Bill held the door open for Shamar that time. He turned the look of displeasure on his face to a smile when his black alligator loafers blessed the smooth pavement outside the car. With the three of them behind him, Shamar walked toward Boogie and stopped a decent distance away from him.

"When you said you wanted to meet, I was hoping you meant a breakfast spot."

"You can do that after you leave here," Boogie said.

"I think you've met Rocko, Major, and Bill," Shamar said, pointing at his entourage.

"I have. My men have been showin' them how we get down in Brooklyn. I hope they're treatin' y'all well."

"If well is lettin' us roll around with 'em without a strap, then hell nah." Rocko's deep voice sounded, and Shamar looked quizzically at Boogie.

"Don't tell me you're letting my most valued men walk around here naked while you're at war."

"They were in good hands," Boogie said. "Plus, you couldn't have really thought I would let them into any of my spots with loaded weapons from jump."

In a sense, Shamar understood Boogie's cautious act, but he still didn't like it.

"What exactly are we doing here, if you don't mind me asking?" he asked.

"Gino," Boogie said to one of the men standing near him. "Show him." He nodded at the well-dressed man to open the slide to the trailer on the back of the semi.

Shamar stood by as he unlatched the door and sent it flying up, revealing a trailer full of guns. Gino took a Glock 19 and showed it to them so they could see the craftsmanship.

"I thought your people might need these," Boogie said to him.

Shamar took the gun from Gino and studied it. He then looked inside the truck and saw many more just like it. Some were small, some bigger, but they were all just regular guns. Although they were nice, they were not what Shamar had in mind.

"Where are the automatic weapons? Explosives?" he asked Boogie. "I thought we would be adequately provided with weapons to defend ourselves."

"That's what those are," Boogie told him. "I'll upgrade your weapons arsenal once you prove yourself to be trustworthy. Until then, these are what your men will move around with in my streets. Is that understood?"

"I think you forget that it's you that needs me," Shamar said, fighting with his upper lip so that it wouldn't curl.

"And I think you forget that we have a deal. If you want me to come through on my end, then you'll do shit my way. No questions asked. Truthfully, if I hadn't made the noise I made the other day, they would remain unstrapped until further notice. That big black motherfucka behind you just rubs me the wrong way."

"I could say the same for you," Major growled behind Shamar.

"Noise? What noise?" Shamar asked, still on the words that had just come from Boogie's mouth.

"You haven't heard? Li, the head of the Chinese family, is dead," Boogie said. "I handled that. So now, my people are on high alert. The Chinese are bound to retaliate at some point, at which time we'll be ready."

"Oh, somebody has been busy."

"I stay busy. Now, grab your shit. I'll send you the lo of where the truck will be later so the rest of your people can get their guns. In the meantime, be on the lookout for anybody who ain't supposed to be in Brooklyn or Staten Island. If you see an unfriendly face, call me before you make any move. Got me?"

Shamar wasn't used to taking orders. He was used to giving them. He knew he was the one who had willingly walked through the door, but he didn't know how much more he could take before he tried to suffocate Boogie.

Shamar's eyes went to the men standing by the Lamborghini. The dissatisfaction must have shown on his face, and he watched as their fingers casually shifted to their trigger fingers. The move was so subtle, but he caught it. Shamar kept his cool, because what Boogie didn't know was that while he stood there like the big man on campus, his own mother was helping plan his demise. Boogie didn't even realize that he was being eaten away at from the inside, and the thought made Shamar smile.

"You got it," Shamar said, and then turned to the men behind him. "Get your guns."

The soft tones of a live violin playing blended in with the sound of glasses clinking all around Shamar as he sifted through tables in an upscale restaurant. The smell of gourmet food invaded his nostrils, and a part of him wished he was there to eat. But he wasn't. He followed closely behind a host, who led him to a table where someone was awaiting his arrival.

"I apologize for my tardiness," he said when he sat down. "I have not stopped moving since I arrived this morning."

"You are here now. That's all that matters," the man sitting across from him said. "But you being late has cut your time with me in less than half."

The man's chair was angled to the point where his top half was in the shadows of the drapes hanging low beside their table. Shamar could barely even make out his face. The vibe he gave off was very ominous, and although it was just the two of them at the table, Shamar bet there were shooters all around, ready to kill him for any wrong move.

"That's fine," Shamar answered. "I won't need much of your time."

"Then don't waste the little of it you have left. You went through a lot to track me down and tell me what's been going on in New York. So, what do you want from me, Shamar Hafford?"

"Guns and explosives. Lots of guns and explosives. And I'll make it worth your while."

Chapter 10

With Boogie sniffing at her tail, Diana didn't think it was safe for her to go see Caesar. However, she called and checked on his condition often. The gunshots had done a great deal of damage, but thankfully, he was getting better with each day that passed. He was still in a coma, but he was safe, and that was all that mattered.

In the meantime, she had two problems on her hands. She had to figure out a way to put the flame on Boogie's ass out and also figure out who had tried to kill Caesar. If it wasn't Boogie, then it had to have been somebody else who had close access to him. In all the decades that Diana had known him, he'd never been so much as grazed by a bullet. The gnawing at the back of her mind got so strong to the point where she couldn't take it anymore.

That same gnawing feeling was what led her to Brooklyn, specifically to the street Big Wheels was on. She knew she would never be able to get video footage from the actual busines because Will, the manager, was loyal to the Tolliver family. Still, Diana's name held weight in some places, and she had loyal friends all over, even in Brooklyn.

Directly across the street from Big Wheels was Johnston's Liquor Store. It was owned by a man in his seventies, Isaac Johnston. Back in his younger days, he used to be one of her father's regular customers. He slowed down on the hookers when he got married, though. Diana caught him a few times in the Sugar Trap, but for the most part, he was a good man. Not only that, but he was a nosey man. If anybody knew anything about something, it was Isaac. See, you found out just as much at a liquor store as you would at a barber shop or hair salon. More, even, since a lot of the people that frequented the liquor store were already drunk with loose lips.

Ding!

The door sounded when Diana pushed it open. A gust of comforting warm air hit her when she stepped inside. She looked around and saw that there were no customers inside and no cashier at the front either.

"Hm," she said, removing a pair of oversized shades from her face. She wondered if he had gone to lunch, but that wouldn't have made sense because the front door was wide open. She listened and heard sounds coming from the back of the building.

The heels on her boots clicked on the ground as she made her way around the counter and to the hallway that led to an office and a storage area. Sure enough, bent over, opening a box with a box cutter was Isaac. His head and his face were full of thick white hair, and he wore a pair of glasses on his nose. She almost chuckled at the overalls and plaid shirt he wore. There was nothing wrong with them; it was just that back in the day, Isaac had been one of the cleanest cats walking the streets. She never would have thought he'd give all of that up, even in his older years, for the grandpa look.

"I was wonderin' when you were gonna show up," he said without looking at her.

"And how do you know who's standing behind you?" she asked.

"You've been wearin' that same perfume since eighty-nine," he said and turned to face her with a serious look on his face. "Also, you're the only one bold enough to come back here unannounced and without permission."

"You know I was never one for rules."

The two stared at each other for a few moments before they both broke out into smiles. Isaac held his arms out, and Diana walked into them. They embraced, and he rubbed her back fondly.

"How are you doing, old friend?" she asked when she pulled away from him.

"Ahh, I could be better." He shook his head. "Barry's boy done lost his damn mind in these streets."

"I heard."

"Well, did you also hear that he's tryna buy us all out on this street?"

"What?" Diana asked, genuinely surprised. "You've been here for over twenty years!"

"Exactly what I said. He's tryna put some sort of shoppin' center over this way."

"That doesn't even sound right." Diana shook her head, but Isaac grabbed a piece of paper from of the metal shelves and handed it to her.

"Read it and weep," Isaac told her. "Some lawyer brought that over here the other day. Boogie wants me to sign my half of the ownership to this place over to him."

"Your half?" Diana asked him, looking over the paper.

"Yeah." Isaac sighed and sat down on one of the boxes behind him. "When I first started this place, I only had half of the money to do it. Barry gave me the other half and became part owner of the business. It was a clean business! He never ran none of his dirty money through here. He knew I wanted to have somethin' honest of my own. He was a good friend. But now his son wants to take it all away from me."

"Because he's now partial owner. Just tell him no, that you don't want to sell."

"I tried to already, and yesterday I found this sitting on the outside of the door!" Isaac reached into the pocket of his overalls and pulled out something shiny. He put it in her hand.

When she reached her hand out, she saw that it was a hollow tip bullet. But it wasn't just a bullet; it was a symbol of a last warning. Diana bit down on her teeth briefly before giving Isaac the bullet.

"How long do you have?"

"Three days," Isaac told her. "Maybe less if anybody saw you walk up in here. Word is, you're not supposed to be on this side of town anymore."

"Yeah, that's the word. But like I said, you know I'm not too good at following rules. Boogie has waged war against the rest of us."

"I thought as much. Especially since he's lettin' those muthafuckas who were just shootin' shit up in Brooklyn move around freely with a pass."

"Wait, what muthafuckas are you talking about?"

"The ones from Ohio. They were up in here earlier today, walkin' around like this was their shit. Boogie is playin' a dangerous game if he's in business with them."

Isaac probably didn't know how much information he'd just given her with that short exchange. Suddenly, a few of the missing lines connected from dot to dot in her head. The only reason Boogie would form a partnership with someone like Shamar, especially after killing his son, was if they were forming an army—one that was big and strong enough to go against the likes of the other four families. It was a smart move, but as Isaac had said, very dangerous. The price Boogie would have to pay would be grave.

Diana couldn't help but to wonder how the two of them had come together, but then she remembered that she'd come to the liquor store for a reason.

"Isaac, I came here to ask you about Caesar," she said.

"You don't have to worry about that," Isaac said, waving his hand. "I won't tell anybody that he's alive."

"W–what?" Diana's eyebrows raised.

"You don't have to play dumb with me. I know. I saw them come and get him out of there. I also saw y'all burn the other boy's body and take his teeth out."

Nobody else besides Li and Marco knew how they'd been able to fake Caesar's death. Julius was listed as a missing person, when really his body was said to have been Caesar's. Diana stumbled to find her words, and when they didn't come out right away, she cleared her throat.

"Isaac . . . you know—"

"I would have said somethin' already if I was ever gonna. I'm also the only brotha over here who was smart enough to get a surveillance system that works! I deleted all of the footage from that night."

"Did you . . . did you see anything on the footage at all?" she asked hopefully.

"Like who shot Caesar? No. I only saw Julius enter Big Wheels with somebody in a black jumpsuit type outfit. Caesar came, and you could hear gunshots. Then Boogie came. He was only there for a short period of time before he left. Not too long after that was when you could hear the last gunshots go off."

"So it could have been Julius who tried to kill Caesar?" Diana asked.

"Or it could have been the person in the black jumpsuit who killed them both." Isaac shrugged. "I deleted the footage right after I saw them walking out of the building. They still had the gun in their hands. I wish my camera was more clear so I could be of more help."

"No, Isaac, you've helped me more than you even know. Thank you."

"No problem. I just wish somebody could help me."

"Nobody's going to take your business from you, I promise you that," Diana told him.

"You just worry about stayin' alive out there. I heard those boys talkin' this mornin' about all the new weapons they just got in. I don't know what Boogie's plannin' on doin', but it ain't good. I just want shit to go back to normal."

"Me too," Diana told him and leaned down to give him a kiss on the forehead. "Give Lisa my love."

"I sure the hell will not! You know that woman is crazy. I'm not even gonna tell her I saw you." Isaac looked alarmed when Diana brought up his wife, and she couldn't help but to laugh.

"She's still the jealous type, I see."

"Worse." Isaac waved goodbye and continued sorting through boxes of liquor.

Before Diana left the building, she checked the surroundings outside. The street was calm, and she didn't see anyone coming her way. Still, she couldn't be too careful. She exited with her shades back on her face and her head down.

Keeping her movements as casual as she could, she walked to the Chevrolet Malibu parked a little way from the building. The passenger door unlocked, and Diana hurried to get inside.

Morgan, who was wearing a black wig with bangs, a trench coat, and a pair of sunglasses, was waiting for her. When Diana told her to dress inconspicuously, she hadn't meant for her to dress like an undercover detective.

"You get the information you came for?" Morgan asked.

"No, not really," Diana answered. "But I did get something else. Head back to the condo."

She'd been staying in a two-story condo in Harlem that she owned off the books, instead of in her own home. Morgan was the only one outside of her trusted shooters who knew it existed. Although her home was protected, Diana preferred to be in a place nobody suspected.

As Morgan drove through Brooklyn, Diana's phone began to ring. She pulled it from her purse and saw that it was Nicky.

"Hello?" she answered.

"I got that information you wanted on your boy Boogie," Nicky said. "He's linked up with—"

"Shamar Hafford," Diana finished for him.

"You already knew?"

"I found out recently that I still have a few friends in enemy territory. You took too long."

"My bad. I've been busy keeping shit in order on this side."

"Is everything all right?"

"Yeah, I got shit handled," he assured her. "What I wanna know is how the two of them got into bed together, especially when Boogie didn't just get his son killed. He did it himself. Somethin' isn't smellin' right with that one."

"They are nothing but enemies that share common interests. They both want to expand, and both have something the other wants. It is a union made from disaster, and we all will pay for it."

"Not if we kill both of them."

The thought of killing Shamar brought Diana much satisfaction, but Boogie, not so much. That was something she would only do if she had to. As clouded as he was at the moment, he was still Barry's son.

"So, what do you want to do?" she heard Nicky ask her, and she snapped back to the conversation.

"We're going to show him exactly why he would rather be with us than against us, and then get those muthafuckas out of New York."

"Sounds like my kind of talk. Just be safe movin' around out here. There are a lot of unfamiliar faces right now."

They said their farewells, and Diana hung up the phone as Morgan stopped at a red light. They were sitting there for a while when a silver truck slowed to a stop next to them. The windows were tinted so dark that Diana couldn't see through them, but when they began to roll down, the hairs on the back of her neck stood up.

Diana's eyes grew wide when she saw the barrels of AR-15 assault rifles point out the windows at the Malibu. She tried to shout for Morgan to drive, but Morgan had already peeped what was going on. She pressed her foot on the gas and ran the light just as the guns started singing. The back windows of the car were blasted out, and the truck chased behind them, firing wildly. Diana was sure some of their bullets hit unintended targets, but that wasn't her concern at the moment.

"Oh my God. Oh my God!" Morgan repeated over and over as she sped.

"Just relax and focus on driving," Diana said in a calm voice. "We're already in the situation. Focus on getting us out of it alive."

"How can I focus on anything when we're getting shot at?" Morgan said and let out a scream when the driver-side mirror was shot off.

"You were just fearless the other night."

"Don't remind me," Morgan said. "Who are they anyway?"

"I didn't see anybody's face, but if I had to guess, I'd say they worked for Boogie."

Diana took a gun out of her purse as Morgan continued to weave in and out of traffic. Morgan looked incredulously at the pistol like it was the silliest thing she'd ever seen.

"A pistol? What is that going to do against those big-ass guns?"

Diana ignored her and looked back at the Suburban. It was gaining on them, and she knew she would have to think fast, or they were both dead. She turned her attention back to the front window and noticed that traffic was lighter in oncoming traffic.

"Roll your window down and let them get closer," she instructed.

"Closer? So they can have better aim to kill us?" Morgan exclaimed but did as she was told.

"Just trust me. When I tell you to, step on it and turn the steering wheel as far left as you can."

"What?"

"Slow down some more." The truck was almost where Diana needed it to be.

"Diana . . ."

"Now!"

Diana braced herself as Morgan turned the steering wheel. The car turned fast, but the world moved in slow motion. Diana aimed her gun at Morgan's open window and waited until the car was at a ninety-degree angle. When she was looking directly at the front of the Suburban, she pulled the trigger twice, sending her bullets directly to the driver's side. The windows were tinted, but she knew she'd hit her intended target when the horn of the truck began blaring and it lost control. She imagined the driver slumped over the steering wheel due to her bullets lodging in his head.

As they jumped over the median and swerved into oncoming traffic, they witnessed the Suburban crashing hard into a pole.

Morgan sat catching her breath while Diana put her gun away and grabbed her phone from the floor. She guessed Boogie was done giving her chances, and the reality that she meant nothing to him hit her the same way the truck had hit the pole. She dialed his number, and he answered on the first ring.

"You must have got the note I left at your door. I ain't think it was gon' take you this long to call, though."

"Yeah, I got the note. I also have the bullets in my car from your men trying to kill me just now. You better call your connects in the feds. You got some bodies to clean up. Wait . . . you probably don't even know you have connects in the feds, do you? You're so busy trying to kill everyone and everything your father worked hard to build. You should be ashamed of yourself, Bryshon Tolliver! But it's okay. I'm going to humble you."

She disconnected the call before he could even get another word in. Truthfully, she wanted to be angrier than she was, but she knew it was risky going to Brooklyn.

For a while, there was nothing but silence in the car. The cold air from Morgan's rolled-down window smacked them in the face, until finally she rolled it up. Diana saw her keep glancing over at her with a look of wonder on her face.

"We have to dump this car," Morgan said, finally finding her voice. "That just happened in front of too many witnesses."

"Smart girl. Hop on the freeway. There is an old junkyard in Manhattan where they know me. They'll take care of the car."

"Okay," Morgan said and merged on the freeway.

As she drove, she continued to sneak glances, until finally Diana rolled her eyes.

"Is there something you want to say?" she asked.

"That . . . that was incredible! Where did you learn to shoot like that?"

"My father taught me to shoot, but Caesar taught me how to aim," Diana answered, checking the rearview mirror. "I may be getting up in age, but survival has no expiration date."

"Will you teach me?"

"If you want to learn."

"You're the one who said I need to keep a gun on me."

"If you have a gun, I guess I just assumed you knew how to shoot." Diana scrunched her forehead up.

"I guess I bought it without ever thinking I was gonna have to use it." Morgan shrugged. "Honestly, I only got it because I started working at the club. Before this, I lived a pretty sheltered life."

"I guess I'm no good for you," Diana told her.

"I wouldn't say that. My parents always made me feel like I had to be perfect, like them. But I'm not like them.

They're boring and never do anything fun. When they found out I wasn't going to finish college, they made me feel like such a failure. Working for you makes me feel like I have a purpose. And today, even though it was scary as hell, was the most excitement I've had in a long time."

"I know I told you to get used to it, but I lied. I will never put you in danger like that again. I shouldn't have even had you drive me today. I should have come alone."

"Please, my driving is what kept us alive today! After you teach me to shoot, we'll make a good team."

Diana didn't know whether to be concerned or to laugh. It was like Morgan hadn't been screaming her head off not even thirty minutes prior. Diana just shook her head and gave her the directions to the junkyard so they could have the car turned into a block.

Chapter 11

Boogie stared at the phone in confusion when Diana disconnected the call. The only move he had okayed was the move in Chinatown. He didn't sign off on anything else, so he had no idea what Diana was talking about, but he planned on getting to the bottom of it.

"Yo, what the fuck was that about?" Bentley's voice sounded.

They'd been standing in the kitchen of Boogie's condo, plotting their next move before Diana called. Boogie had been staying in his condo for the last few days as an attempt to keep Roz out of his business. He knew from their last conversation that she just wouldn't understand, so he felt it was best to keep his distance and tap in with her when he could.

"Did you give the order for anybody to clap at Diana?"

"Nah. Why? What happened?"

"Diana just said somebody just got at her in traffic."

"It couldn't have been any of our boys. They know not to move like that without the say so. You better check with that nigga Shamar. No cap, them niggas just seem a little greasy to me."

Before Boogie could respond, his phone went off again.

"Talk to me."

"Aye, you heard what just happened?" Tazz's voice came from the other end. "There was a shootout not too far away from Big Wheels. It's bad. I don't know who they were shooting at, but they got fucked up in the process. Two bodies are dead inside their truck, but we got the other three who were responsible with us right now."

"Are they ours?" Boogie asked.

"Kind of. These are the muthafuckas your friend sent from Ohio. I thought these niggas were supposed to be smart. Shooting in traffic—in broad daylight, might I add—is *not smart*!"

"Take 'em to Staten Island. I'ma handle it. What about the other bodies?" Boogie asked.

"Being dumped somewhere as we speak."

"A'ight, I'ma see you in a few."

"No doubt."

"I guess we're headed to Staten Island then," Bentley commented when Boogie hung up the phone.

"I'ma fuck Shamar up for this!" Boogie bellowed.

"So they *were* his niggas?"

"Yeah. Tazz got em right now. Let's go so I can get to the bottom of this."

He grabbed his car keys and the two of them made to leave. They didn't get too far, though, because when Boogie opened the front door, he was confronted by Roz. There was a fire in her eyes that he had never seen before, and instantly he was concerned.

"Baby, what's wrong? Where's Amber?" Boogie asked as she stormed inside the condo.

"Is it true?" Roz asked, ignoring his questions. "Is it true!"

"Is what true?" Boogie asked, outwardly confused.

"This!"

Roz shoved her phone in his face so that he could read the screen. It was open on an article from that day about a restaurant explosion. Li's face was plastered all over the page, and the article named many other casualties. Boogie looked away from the phone and back at Roz's angry face.

"Did you do it?" She asked, and when Boogie turned his head away, she snatched it back to face her. "I asked you a question, nigga. Did you kill these people?"

"Why are you askin' questions you don't really wanna know the answer to?" he asked, and her eyes widened.

"I thought you set a meeting to talk to them to make peace."

"Then you assumed, and you assumed wrong," Boogie said bluntly. "I told you what type of time I was on. He was just in the way."

"Just in the way? Do you hear yourself right now?" Roz asked incredulously at his nonchalant attitude. She turned to Bentley, who was just as nonchalant, and said, "You were with him, weren't you?"

"Roz, just go home, a'ight? We can talk about this later," Bentley said in a dismissive tone, but that didn't do anything but make her angrier.

"There might not be a later! You can't just go around killin' people and thinkin' they won't fire back at you!"

"I know what I'm doin'," Boogie said.

"I don't think you do." Roz shook her head at him. "You are not the man I fell in love with. You're different."

"Change is somethin' that should be expected with everything."

"Not like this. You've let your anger completely consume you. It says thirty people were killed, Boogie!"

"You knew what kind of man I was when you met me!" Boogie barked, and Roz's eyes grew wide.

He'd never raised his voice at her before, and he instantly regretted it after seeing the hurt in her eyes. She blinked away her tears and took a breath.

"Until the man I know comes back, you are not welcome around me or my child. You either, Bentley. My daughter and I will not be a part of this game of slaughter that you're playing. You're both gon' get yourselves killed."

"Roz, baby. Wait." Boogie tried to grab her arm.

"Are you gon' stop doin' what you're doin' and come home?" Roz asked.

Boogie couldn't answer the way she wanted him to because he didn't want to lie to her face. "Roz . . . I can't."

"Then I can't wait. I could deal with who you were before, but this? No. It's over, Boogie."

The disappointed expression she wore on her face as she walked away was one he would never forget. When she was gone, he was frozen. It felt like he'd just gotten her, and just that fast, he lost her.

Bentley gave him a comforting pat on the shoulder. "I know my sister, and she's serious," Bentley told him.

"I shouldn't be with anyone who doesn't understand the life I live." Boogie pretended to not be phased. "Come on. We gotta go."

They finally left, but Roz's words were on his mind the entire ride to Staten Island. He knew that he was a different person, but was she right when she said he'd let anger consume him? He had grown so accustomed to walking around with it that it had just become normal. What Roz didn't understand was that it would be almost impossible to go back to being the old him. His anger was born from pain, and if he let go of the anger, all that would be left was hurt. There was no room for that in his life.

When they arrived at the spot in Staten Island, Boogie took note that there were no more bullet holes or blood stains in the lounge. The walls were freshly painted, and a new pool table had been brought in. Boogie decided Bosco had been on to something with the red carpet, so he kept it. Tazz was already there, waiting for him with the men responsible for the shootout. They stood by the pool table and stared defiantly at Boogie when he entered.

Boogie took one look at the men and recognized them as Shamar's shooters, Major, Rocko, and Bill. He had met them briefly and found out they were brothers. When he met them and the others Shamar had sent, Boogie had provided them with weapons. He also gave them the rundown on who was and wasn't allowed in Brooklyn. If they saw any of them, they were to let him know, and he would tell them what to do.

The three of them put him in the mind of the rap group Migos from the way they dressed and the locs in their hair. They were unarmed, and standing around them were Boogie's own shooters, ready to blow their heads off at any moment.

Boogie's gaze went to the pool table, where three AR-15 assault rifles were lying, and he raised a brow. "These ain't the guns Gino gave y'all," Boogie said, referring to Bentley's cousin.

Gino had helped them take down Shane Hafford not too long ago and had committed to providing Boogie with high-grade weapons ever since. What had started out shaky had proved to be a promising relationship, given the fact that Boogie wouldn't be able to buy guns from Marco any longer.

"That's what we found in the truck when we grabbed them," Tazz told him. "They claim they brought them when they travelled, but that's a lie. They flew in. Ain't no way they're letting you three criminal-looking muthafuckas on a plane with not one, but *three* ARs."

"Right," Boogie said and glowered at Shamar's shooters.

He paced in front of them before he stopped in front of the tallest one, Bill. The other two were fair-skinned, while he was black as night. He also had the hardest looking face out of all of them. Boogie could tell just by the coldness in his eyes that the world had hardened him.

"Who the fuck gave you clearance to make such a big scene in my territory?" Boogie asked him.

"We were just following our orders," Bill said smugly.

"Whose orders?"

"Yours, nigga," Bill sneered.

Strike one, Boogie thought, and then backhanded Bill with his pistol because there was only one strike to give. The blow came with a powerful force, and Bill stumbled to the side. His brothers flinched to help, but the sound of guns cocking filled the air. When Bill regained his footing, he went to spit his blood out, but Boogie lifted his chin with the butt of the gun.

"Swallow it. I just got my carpets redone," Boogie said and waited to hear the sound of Bill swallowing. When he did, he continued. "I never gave any of you niggas the okay to do any of the wild shit you did today. You tryna have law enforcement on my ass or somethin'? Is that it? Because it sure seems like it."

"We saw the bitch whose photo you showed us, and we tried to hawk her down," Bill growled. "Ain't that what we're here for?"

"You were supposed to hit me up before you made a decision like that. This is my city. Mine! I call the shots in this bitch! This ain't fuckin' Ohio where you muthafuckas can do what you want. I will fuckin' end you!" Boogie bellowed in Bill's face.

Boogie transformed into a monster in front of Bill, and it was the first time Boogie saw fear flicker in his eyes. Boogie couldn't explain where the jolt of rage he felt had just come from. He didn't know if he was mad at the fact that they hadn't followed his orders, or if it was the fact that they had gone after Diana. The confusion from that made him even angrier, and he commenced to hitting Bill repeatedly with his gun until his face was completely bloody. When he dropped to the ground, Boogie looked loathingly down at him before turning to his goons.

"Since these niggas like dressin' alike, give them all matchin' faces," he instructed, and his men wasted no time getting to it.

As they were being beat to a pulp, Boogie nodded his head, motioning for Bentley to follow him to the bar. Boogie went behind it to the sink to rinse his bloody hands and gun off.

"You straight?" Bentley asked.

"I'm good," Boogie said, drying his hand. "I have a job for you."

"Speak on it."

"I need you to take those guns to Gino and see if he knows where these niggas got them from. Take Tazz with you."

"A'ight. Where you finna be?"

"Brooklyn. I need to figure out what exactly Diana was doin' there in the first place."

Chapter 12

"You have reached the voicemail box of—"

Bentley hung up before the recording could finish speaking. The was the third time that Roz had ignored his call. Frustrated, he tossed the phone into the passenger seat of his car. He was parked in the empty parking lot of a closed fried chicken restaurant in Brooklyn while waiting for Gino. He was taking forever, so Bentley figure he'd try to make amends before Roz's anger stuck. He hadn't seen her as mad as she was earlier that day in a long time. She hadn't gone off like that since Amber's birth father had walked out on her when she was first born. At that time, Bentley had been the one there to comfort her. Now that she had cut him off too, along with Boogie, Bentley didn't know who was there to wipe her tears. He hated when she was angry at him, but she would understand soon why so many sacrifices had to be made. And even if she didn't, they were siblings, so she would have to forgive him eventually. Boogie, on the other hand, was a whole different ball game.

Roz had always been headstrong when it came to men. She was the kind of woman who knew herself and would always choose her peace over anything else. He hoped they would get it together, though. He could tell the two of them really cared about each other, and he knew Boogie had gotten to be attached to Amber.

Bentley picked up his phone and told himself he was going to try her line one more time before he just left her alone. The phone rang three times before he heard it pick up.

"Why do you keep callin' me?" Roz answered with an attitude.

"You left the condo kind of angry, and I was just checkin' to see if you were okay."

"I would be better if you stopped callin' my phone like a bill collector."

"I just don't want you to be mad at me," Bentley said, and he heard her sigh into the phone.

"I just worry about you, a'ight? You're my brother. Besides my daughter, you're the only immediate family that I have. I don't want anything to happen to you while you're out in the streets."

"You don't gotta worry about me. I'ma be a'ight. You gotta trust that and put good vibes out into the universe for me."

"How am I supposed to do that when I see shit like I saw today? Come on, Bentley. What the hell are you doin'? First it was the greedy robberies, and now you and Boogie are on some kingpin shit. We have enough money!"

"Enough money isn't enough money. Because what happens when you're not makin' money? You're spendin' it," Bentley told her.

"Then get a regular job! There are other ways."

"Do you know who you're talkin' to right now? I'm a street nigga, Roz. Same as Boogie. You know this. There ain't no other way for people like us. Do you remember what it was like growin' up without havin' shit? Because I do, and I ain't never goin' back to that. Ever."

"I just feel like Boogie is takin' you down the wrong path because he doesn't know how to sort out his emotions."

"With or without Boogie, I was already on this path. And if we're technically speakin', some of this shit would have never happened if I didn't talk him into doin' robberies off the books. It's true he has a lot of anger in him right now, but so would anybody who was feelin' the shit that he is. The only difference is that he's in the position to do somethin' about it. And I'm in the position right next to that."

"Whatever," Roz said dismissively.

"I hope you know you sound real selfish right now."

"Me? Selfish. Psych!"

"You are. Boogie is the same nigga he was before. He just had to turn his savage up. For one second, think about somebody other than yourself. The streets would eat him up alive if he wasn't a monster, and you know that. If you loved him, and if you loved me, you would accept that. He accepted you, and you came with the baggage of a whole baby."

"Oh, so now my daughter is baggage. Did he say that?" Roz asked with hurt in her voice.

"No, don't twist my words," Bentley said and sighed. "All I'm sayin' is did he ever once make you feel like less of a woman just because you have a child? Matter of fact, Roz, you don't even have a job!"

"Because you always took care of me."

"And that's all Boog is tryna do," he told her.

"Whatever," Roz said, and he could hear the smile in her tone.

"So you gon' take us back?"

"Us?"

"Hell yeah. You just tried to cut me off from seein' my niece! That ain't right!"

"I guess I can take you back because you're my brother, we're blood. But Boogie . . . I don't know. Maybe when he works through what he needs to work through."

"A'ight, just don't make him body a nigga behind you. Because he will." At that moment, Bentley saw the person he was waiting for pull up beside him. "Roz, I'ma hit you back. Gino just pulled up."

He disconnected the phone and unlocked his car doors so Gino could get in. As usual, Gino was dressed very dapper and had a fresh haircut. The strong kush aroma coming from his pea coat hit Bentley's nose when Gino shook his hand.

"What's good, cuz?" Bentley greeted him.

"Shit, tryna see what was so important that I had to leave my bitch to come meet you. She already been on my neck crazy, thinkin' I have another bitch somewhere."

"And do you?"

"Nigga you *know* I have another bitch! But if I'ma catch hell behind her, I would rather actually have been with her. You feel me?"

"I feel you," Bentley said, laughing. "Nigga, you ain't never gon' change."

"The only thing constant with me is business. What's good with you, though? I saw you hang up fast as hell when I got to the car."

"Man, that was just Roz. She trippin'."

"Baby cuz been trippin' since we were little. Anyways, what's goin' on?" Gino asked and got comfortable in his seat.

"You know the niggas you loaded up with weapons? The ones from Ohio."

"Yeah, I gave them niggas Glocks like Boogie told me to."

"Then how the fuck did they get their hands on these?" Bentley pulled one of the AR-15s from the back seat. "If they didn't get them from you, and we're almost certain that they didn't get them from Marco, where did they get them from?"

He handed it to Gino, who looked at it with the eyes of someone peering down at their favorite thing in the world. He held the assault rifle up to his face and studied it closely. His fingers traced it carefully, almost as if he were looking for something.

"This weapon was made from scratch. There is no serial number. But there is something else here. A name on the handle. Morty."

"Morty? Is there a Morty in New York who makes guns?"

"I don't know," Gino said truthfully. "But I can find out."

"Good, because Boogie needs you to figure out who's selling Shamar weapons under his nose."

"I don't know why your boy is doin' business with him anyways. I wouldn't trust anybody if I was the one who murdered their son."

"Boogie is a smart man. He knows what he's doin'," Bentley told him and took the weapon from him. "We just need you to handle that for us."

He wrapped the gun back up in the blanket the other two were in and gave them all to Gino. When Gino got out and got back into his own vehicle, Bentley waited for him to leave before he drove off in the opposite direction.

Chapter 13

For the life of him, Boogie couldn't understand why Diana had chanced coming to Brooklyn, knowing things weren't sweet between their camps. When Tazz said the shootout happened not too far away from Big Wheels, Boogie figured that was the first place he should stop. Upon his arrival, he saw his mother's Jeep already parked outside. He wondered what she was doing there, especially since she hadn't returned any of his calls in days.

When Boogie stepped out of the car, the brisk cold nipped at his ears, so he popped the collar of his coat. After he walked through the front door of the business, he wiped his loafers on the mat by the front door and peered around. There was one person sitting in the waiting area, reading a car magazine, and Boogie could hear the mechanics hard at work in the garage. Will, the manager, was typing something into the computer behind the front desk. However, he stopped everything he was doing when he noticed Boogie walk through.

"Well, if it isn't the big boss in charge. Looking just like your father!" he exclaimed, reaching over the counter to shake Boogie's hand. "I was just about to shoot our books over to the accountant."

"How is everything?" Boogie asked.

"Whew, honestly? Better, much better. For a while there, business had slowed. I guess since this was the place where they found Caesar's body, muthafuckas didn't want to have shit to do with us. Until they realized nobody else fixes or details like us!"

"Fa sho!" Boogie nodded. "I have a question, Will, and be honest with me."

"Ask away, boss man."

"Was Diana here?"

"Nah, I haven't seen her since you said she wasn't permitted around these parts. But when I really think about it, I ain't really seen her in a while. Not since Barry died."

"Okay." Boogie took in his words, trying to decide if he believed him.

"Why do you ask?" Will looked curiously at him. "Does this have anything to do with that shootout? The shit's all over the news."

"Maybe. Anyway, I saw my mother's car outside. She here?"

"Actually, she's in one of the offices in the back."

"Thanks."

Boogie let him finish doing what he was doing and headed to the back. He figured he would find her in his office, since it had once been his father's, but when he passed Julius's office, he saw her sitting at the desk. She didn't see him standing in the doorway at first. He studied her. She was beautiful and wearing her usual two-piece suit, but Dina looked sad. She traced the edges of the desk softly with her hands and sighed.

"Am I interrupting anything, or do you want some more alone time with that desk?" Boogie asked, startling her.

"Boogie! Oh I–I didn't see you there," she said, jumping to her feet. "I was just admiring the craftsmanship of the wood. Your father did always have good taste. He chose the furnishings in this entire building, you know."

"I didn't know that. I guess I just thought he hired somebody to do that," Boogie said as she approached him.

She gave him a hug before stepping past him and going farther down to Barry's office. Boogie was close behind her as she opened the door and flicked the switch. The first place she went was to a tall file cabinet in the corner.

"I came here to find the deeds to those businesses across the street. Once I have them, I can hire a construction company to demolish the buildings so they can start building my outlet mall.

"We and our," Boogie corrected her while she rummaged through files.

"What's that you said?" she asked.

"Once *we* have them, *we* can hire a construction company to tear down the buildings and they can start building *our* outlet mall."

"That's what I said, son." Dina pulled a folder out of the cabinet. "Aha! Here they are."

She sat down in the desk chair and thumbed through the thick folder. The triumphant smile on her face grew smaller and smaller with each paper she looked at. By the time she got to the last one, her mouth was formed in a frown.

"These are the deeds to all of his businesses. Every single last one of them. They have your name on them."

"Yeah, they all got reworked after Pops died. His will was honored. But that shouldn't be a problem. I'll give you whatever information you need."

"Great."

"What's wrong, Mama?" Boogie asked, hearing the briskness in her tone.

"That man really didn't leave me a thing. Not a house, not a business. Nothing. Even my cars are in your name. You would think after all the years we spent together . . . He didn't appreciate me. That's why I . . ." Her voice faded, and her eyes stared off into space.

"That's why you what, Mama?"

"That's why I just want to put something up of my own. Those buildings across the street look so old and run down anyway," she finished, blinking her eyes and turning her gaze to him. "What did you come down here for?"

"Just seein' how things are goin' around here," he lied.

"I heard about what happened to Li. I'm proud of you. One down, two more to go. You are fearless. Soon, the boroughs will be united under one. You."

"I just have to keep things smooth in my camp between my people, the Italians, and Shamar."

"Shamar?" Dina closed the folder in her lap. "How are things going with the two of you working together?"

"It's already startin' off bad. I'm beginnin' to think accepting his help was a mistake. I think he's calling shots that I didn't authorize already."

"Oh, son. He just started working under you. He'll fall in line."

"Nah, he should have come already in line."

"You have to take into consideration that where he's from, he's king."

"Well, here he ain't nothin' but a runner. He has one more time to do some shit I don't like."

"What did he do?"

"Sent some of his shooters after Diana."

Dina's face twitched at the sound of her name. Her lip turned up, and she stood from the chair. Her eyes pierced his like daggers.

"Isn't that what they're here for? Taking down the other families was the reason you brought them here," she said.

"What they did wasn't calculated. They shot at her in broad daylight."

"And you killed Li in front of tons of witnesses. What's the difference?"

"That I'm the boss, and I call the shots."

"No." Dina shook her head with a chuckle. "That's not what this is about. This is about *her*. You don't want anything to happen to her, do you?"

"What this is about is moves bein' made without my consult," Boogie said, ignoring her question.

"I hope so," Dina said through pursed lips. "Your weakness for her will be the reason you're lying in a pool of your own blood. Do you understand me?"

She didn't wait for him to answer because she stormed out of the room. Her last words lingered in the air. She was right. If Diana thought that he was the one that had sent shooters after her, then she would not hold back the next time he saw her. He had to tighten up and let go of whatever soft spot he had for her.

He sighed and sat down in the same seat Dina had been sitting in. He realized that she left the folder of deeds behind in her upset. Boogie made a mental note to drop them off to her later.

As he powered on the computer, he thought back to Will saying Diana hadn't been there in a while. The reason why Boogie wondered if he was telling the truth was simple. Diana had been on that side of town for a reason, and he had no doubt that she still had loyal friends all over New York, even in Brooklyn. There was only one way to find out.

When the computer was on, Boogie clicked on Big Wheels' front desk security footage from that day. He rewound it to when they opened and played it through in a time lapse. As it turned out, Will had been telling the truth. Diana hadn't been there at all.

"Hmm," he said and tapped his finger on the desk.

He was about to shut the computer off when something told him to check the outside cameras. It was a long shot, but he did it anyway. He also rewound those recordings to the beginning of the day and let them play through. As he watched, his eyes fell on a Malibu that was parked across the street at Johnston's Liquor Store. That wasn't the strange part, since it was a liquor store that got customers all the time. What stood out to him was the woman wearing sunglasses with her head tucked down, walking from the car inside the business. He rewound the tape again. That time, he froze the screen on her at the moment right before she tucked her head down, and he zoomed in.

"There you are," he said, getting up from the desk.

He grabbed the folder from the desk and left the office and headed for the front door. Boogie barely heard Will say goodbye when he walked out. He was too focused. Before he crossed the street, he put the folder in his car and locked the doors. He should have known that it was Isaac that Diana had come to see, especially since he was the only one to give him and his mother a hard time about the business. Boogie's father had given Isaac fifty percent ownership of the liquor store, which was making it a real pain for Boogie. Without Isaac's cooperation, the shopping center couldn't happen.

Ding!

The door chime was loud when Boogie entered. He spotted Isaac at the front. It seemed that he had just finished ringing a customer out and was about to help another. Boogie cut everyone and stood at the front of the line.

When Isaac saw him, one would have thought he had a nasty taste in his mouth the way that he looked at Boogie.

"You," he growled.

"Me," Boogie confirmed and turned to the people behind him. "We're closed."

They took one look at him and didn't argue. He watched as they scrambled out of the building. Some put the things in their hands back; some didn't. Boogie went to the door and flipped the OPEN sign t o CLOSED so nobody else would walk in. He went back to the counter so he could be face to face with the glaring old man.

"You can't just come in here messin' with my business like that!" Isaac exclaimed, pointing a finger at Boogie.

"Last I checked, I owned half this business," Boogie said. "You know why I'm here, Isaac?"

"About that damned shoppin' center you keep goin' on and on about. Well, I'm not sellin' out! Boy, you're gon' have to kill me if you want my half of the business. Your father would never do anything like this!"

"We can discuss all of that later, but that's not really what I'm here about."

"Then what the hell you want, boy? To raise my blood pressure some more?" Isaac asked, growing more impatient by the second.

Boogie was letting his rudeness slide. He'd known Isaac since he was a kid. However, he wasn't going to be too many more "boys."

"Tell me why Diana was here," Boogie said bluntly, and the fire in Isaac extinguished immediately.

"I don't know what you're talkin' about. Diana ain't been here."

Isaac wiped his hands on his overalls and went to stocking some cigarettes behind the counter. Suddenly, he was avoiding Boogie's eye contact, and it was obvious.

"I don't like when people lie to me," Boogie said. "I know she was here. I just need to know why."

"Like I said, Diana ain't been here. Now, you should just go on and attend to whatever business needs attendin'!"

"I watched the security footage from across the street. She was here."

Boogie showed his hand, figuratively speaking, and now there was no way Isaac could deny the fact. Isaac stopped doing what he was doing and was silent. Boogie could tell that he was trying to decide his next course of action. Finally, the old man sighed and looked at Boogie through the glasses on his nose.

"Yeah, she was here."

"Weren't you told like all of the other business owners around here that she wasn't allowed around this way?"

"Muthafucka, do you think I'ma listen to the rules of a boy who doesn't even know what he's doin'? Kiss my ass. Diana is an old friend of mine. She'll always be welcome here."

Boogie bit the inside of his cheek. Isaac was an old school G. There was nothing Boogie could do that would intimidate him. That much was apparent.

"Why did she come see you, of all people?"

"Didn't I say she's an old friend of mine?" Isaac asked, but then Boogie cut his eyes at him. "Fine, but first let me tell you that you don't scare me. Now, your father? That was a bad muthafucka."

"Can you just tell me what I want to know? You're wastin' both of our time."

"She wanted to see the security footage from my camera from the night Caesar was . . . killed."

"Did you show her?" Boogie asked curiously.

He hadn't thought to come ask Isaac for his recording of that night.

"Couldn't." Isaac shrugged. "I deleted the footage from that entire day."

"And why would you do that?"

"I'm an old school cat. We don't keep any incriminating evidence just in case the feds come sniffing their noses."

"Okay, but you must have watched it before you deleted it," Boogie said. "You must have told her something."

"I'ma tell you like I told her. All I saw was Julius walk in with somebody, then Caesar, then you."

"Wait. There wasn't anybody with Julius," Boogie said, thinking back.

He remembered because he was there. It had only been him, Julius, and Caesar. Nobody else was in Big Wheels that night.

"I assure you there was. And the two of you were the only ones who walked out."

Isaac had a "matter of fact" expression on his face.

It suddenly clicked in Boogie's head. The person he spoke of must have been the one who killed Caesar.

"Did you get a good look at this person's face?"

"No. He was wearing one of those sweatsuits, black. The hood was over his face."

"A black sweatsuit?" Boogie's brow raised.

"Yup. I wish I still had the video. All I can tell you for sure is he was short. Kind of petite. Maybe it was one of these young bucks out here tryna get some street cred."

"No. I don't think so."

His mind flashed back to that same night at his condo. When his mother had come to see him, she had been wearing a black sweat suit. Maybe it was just a coincidence, but if so, it was a hell of a coincidence. Especially since that wasn't her usual clothing choice.

He could admit she had been acting strange ever since his father was murdered, from trying to sell off his properties right away and then goading him into starting a war. He'd just chalked it up to her being in as much pain as he was. But what if it was something else?

He knew she wasn't fond of Caesar, but could she really have killed him? He was having a hard time picturing Dina as a murderer. Maybe she knew he was the one that killed her husband, but why wouldn't she have told Boogie? There were too many questions coming to his mind that he didn't have any of the answers he needed to know.

"Thank you, Isaac."

"Mm-hmm," the old man grumbled. "Now get out of my store."

Boogie felt as if he were in a daze as he walked back across the street to his vehicle. The weight on his shoulders needed to be lifted immediately. He had to know the truth, and the only way to do that was to confront his mother.

He was about to get inside his car when two trucks sped into the parking lot of Big Wheels and skidded to a stop behind him. Boogie didn't even have time to pull his gun from his hip before the doors of both SUVs swung open and ten men hopped out. Multiple red dots appeared on his chest from their guns being pointed at him, and he groaned loudly.

"What a fuckin' day."

Chapter 14

Earlier that day

The aroma of a burning Cuban cigar filled the air as Nicky took a long drag. He was seated in Caesar's extravagant basement in one of his luxury recliners. The spacious basement could be considered another house being that there was a kitchen, sitting area, two bedrooms, and two bathrooms. It was so quiet down there that it could have been perceived that he was alone. But he wasn't. The highest ranked members of his family stood around him in the sitting area.

Nicky had just hung up with Diana and told everyone to be silent while he traveled through his own thoughts. As the new boss in Manhattan, Nicky had some decisions to make. There was a true threat in New York that needed to be extinguished. He didn't know Boogie personally, but that would make the job easier to be done.

The crazy thing was that the five family heads hadn't changed in decades, and when they finally did, war broke out. He didn't understand how Boogie didn't see that he was the cause of the disorder. His thirst for power was making things worse for everybody. What Diana had said was true. Without management, no business could function.

"Caesar is gone," Nicky started when he finally spoke again. "And I know there are some muthafuckas who don't respect that I'm in charge now. I need y'all to make sure they feel me, understand?"

"Understood," the men in the room said in unison.

"Fa sho," Nathan, Nicky's younger brother, who stood the closest to him, said and nodded his head. "They already know how I'm comin' if they disrespect you."

Nathan was five years younger than Nicky and a hot-head, which made him the perfect soldier. His skin was the color of peanut butter, and he rocked a short fade. He kept his face clear of any hair, and that would have given him a cute baby face if it weren't for all of his battle scars. He'd been getting into fights since he was only five years old, and Nicky couldn't remember a time when he'd lost. He would do whatever it took to win, no matter the cost.

"I'm already knowing," Nicky told him. "But besides the shit goin' on in our camp, right now we have a problem that's fuckin' up the way we normally do business, and we need to solve it. Boogie has to get put down like a dog. Diana feels—"

"Man, cuz, *fuck* what Diana feels." Jerrod, Nicky's cousin, spoke up. "If you want muthafuckas to feel you, we need to handle this shit ourselves without the other families. The old ways are dyin' out."

"I hate to admit it, but Jerrod is right," Nicky's other cousin Dennis said. "Caesar's death hit the streets the hardest, which means we look the weakest. That nigga has been able to move and groove too long. He shoulda *been* in the dirt."

"Hell yeah. Especially now since he's lettin' outsiders in our shit. That ain't never happened before. It's out of hand, cuz." Jerrod shook his head, and the room erupted with cosigning.

"Shut the fuck up!" Nicky commanded briskly, and they all grew quiet. "Jerrod, let me be the first to say that if you ever interrupt me again, you gon' regret that shit, my boy. The only way that the old ways will die out is if we continue to disregard them. There already is a nigga out there movin' rogue. We don't need another."

"Yeah, niggas. Y'all need to give him the same respect you would if he were Caesar." Nathan spoke up for his brother.

"He ain't Caesar, though," Jerrod said, taking a challenging step toward Nathan.

"Exactly. He's Nicky King, bitch," Nathan said and brandished his pistol. "Matter of fact, you don't even carry our last name, because your mama was a ho. My uncle ain't even know if you was his. The only reason he claimed you was because of Caesar. So, if I was to kill you right now, ask me if I would give a fuck."

He pointed the gun at Jerrod's head and stared at him with his crazy eyes. They looked crazy because one of them was bigger than the other, and he held them both open as wide as they would go. Everybody there knew that Nathan was the Mad Max of them all.

Jerrod looked at Nathan and at the gun before stepping back. "Aye, yo, Nathan. You're trippin'. I was just sayin'—"

"My brother didn't ask you to say shit, bitch!" Nathan barked and looked slowly around the room. When it seemed that they were all in check, he gave the mic back to Nicky, but he never put his gun away. "Go ahead and finish talkin', bro."

"I was sayin' that Diana feels like it's time to hit Boogie from all sides. I think we should take a play from his own book."

"What you mean?" Nathan asked.

"You heard what he did to the Chinese motherfucka? At his own shit? Well, I say we take a trip to Brooklyn. He won't be expectin' it. And if he is, he'll get the message that we aren't afraid to bring the game to his playground."

They all were nodding at his words, including Jerrod. He was finally speaking their language. It was Nicky's first true test of being the boss in charge, and thanks to Nathan, he seemed to have passed.

"What do you need us to do?" Dennis asked.

"I need you and Jerrod to snuff the nigga out. When you spot him, call me."

"Yup," Jerrod said and waved his hand for their other cousins to follow him.

Shortly after they made their exit, everybody else besides Nathan and Nicky did too. When they were gone, Nicky put out the cigar between his fingers and set it down in an ashtray. He was quiet as he was once again lost in his thoughts.

"I know that look," Nathan commented and took a seat in one of the luxury recliners in the basement. He leaned back and made himself comfortable and glanced over at Nicky. "Your brain is workin' overtime."

"I just I have this feeling gnawin' at the back of my head right now. Thanks for havin' my back. I guess havin' a crazy-ass baby brother pays off, huh?"

"You damn right."

"You ain't have to call his mama a ho, though," Nicky said, and the two exchanged a look and burst out laughing.

"I was just statin' facts! Like, how you gon' talk crazy and we don't even know if you're blood or not? He better be happy he got a seat at the table to begin with."

Nathan reached for a blunt that was dangling on his ear and lit it with a lighter he pulled from his skinny jeans. All it took was a few puffs for his face to be encircled by a cloud of smoke. If Nicky hadn't quit, he would have asked him to pass it. He was just about to lean back in his chair when Nathan started talking again.

"Don't let that nigga or any of these niggas get to you, though," he said with lungs full of smoke. He exhaled and gave his brother a reassuring look. "They're just mad because it's you and not them. Everybody know that we were Unc's favorites. And we all know his legacy wasn't gon' get passed down to my hothead ass. We would all be dead."

"You stupid." Nicky laughed.

"You know it's true. I never could get a hold of my anger. That's why I smoke to calm my nerves. You were always the best pick, not just because you got a savage lurkin' in you, but because you know how to tame it. I know one thing, though."

"What?"

"You gotta accept the fact that Unc ain't comin' back. I feel like you're still waitin' for him to walk through the doors at any moment. You gotta let that shit go. Handle yours. Caesar built this shit for us. Now you need to run it how you want. That's one thing I admire about Boogie. That nigga made his shit his own. It's time for you to do the same thing."

"So you're sayin' I should do away with the pact and step away from the other families?"

"I'm sayin' the pact been dead since Barry hit the dirt. Then Caesar, and now Li. I feel like you're tryna walk the same line that got them niggas smoked. New don't always mean bad."

Those words echoed in Nicky's head. In that moment, his respect level for Nathan went up a notch, not only because he addressed Nicky with his true thoughts privately, but because when he wanted to, he made more sense than even he knew. In all honesty, Caesar and Nathan were the only ones in the world that Nicky respected highly. It was because the face they wore to the public was who they really were. There was never a façade. A person who had to pretend to be something he wasn't was one who feared what others thought of him, and that was a person that Nicky didn't need around him.

Nathan smoked the rest of his blunt and stood up to leave, but Nicky stopped him.

"Bro."

"What's good? I was finna go link up with Jerrod and them," Nathan said.

"I got somethin' else I need you to do for me."

"Man, you just don't want me in on any action."

"Actually, I do. It's the vault. I need you to move it."

The vault was what they called the resting place of all of their drugs before they were ready to be moved. Before Caesar's death, the only people who knew about it were the highest ranked, but now that he was gone, there was no telling if the information of its location was leaked. That meant that a new place for it would have to be found.

"Nigga, how the fuck am I supposed to move a whole building?" Nathan asked, looking befuddled.

"Not the literal building, you stupid—"

"I'm just fuckin' with you." Nathan grinned. "I'll get on that shit right now."

"A'ight," Nicky said, and they slapped hands. "Stay dangerous."

"Oh, fa sho."

When Nathan was gone, Nicky was alone. He tried to stay out of his thoughts and in the present. He looked around the basement of the house and smiled, knowing that Caesar would have been pissed if he knew Nathan was down there smoking, especially before handling business. He always wanted their minds to be sharp at all times.

Nicky failed at staying in the present as he began remembering all of the good times he'd had with Caesar. He was really his cousin, but he'd taken both Nicky and Nathan in as his nephews when they were just boys. He helped their mother raise them when his first cousin, their father, died. He taught them how to ride their first bikes and how to shoot their first guns. He let them be themselves without altering them in any way, and his love was always genuine.

Nicky was lost in his own mind so deeply that he barely heard his phone ring beside the ashtray on the coffee table. He picked it up and realized that four hours had passed. He had no idea that he'd zoned out for that long. Jerrod's number was on his screen, and Nicky answered before he hung up.

"What's the word?"

"We found him. He just walked into a liquor store outside of where Caesar was killed. You want us to make a move?"

"Nah. Not yet. Not without me."

Chapter 15

Boogie narrowed his eyes at the guns pointed at his head. When the cars had first pulled up, he just knew it was the Chinese coming to get their revenge, but it wasn't. It was Caesar's people. Boogie recognized a few of them, but one in particular stood out. The look on his face told Boogie that he was out for blood.

"You on the wrong side of the tracks, don't you think so, Nicky?" he asked Caesar's nephew.

Boogie didn't know much about Nicky besides the fact that he might have hung out with him a few times as a child. The only thing he knew were the words that blew with the wind of the street, and what they said was that Nicky was a gangster through and through. He and his wild brother were said to be Caesar's most skilled assassins.

"Nah." Nicky shook his head and took a step forward. "I'm supposed to be wherever you're at."

"Is that right?"

"It is."

"State your business then, so I can bounce. I have shit to do."

His words caught Nicky off guard. He looked from Boogie and then to the guns in his people's hands just to make sure they both were seeing the same thing. He chuckled at the look of boredom on Boogie's face.

"Nigga, you ain't goin' nowhere," he said. "You've been a bad motherfucka. Blowin' shit up. Killin' my partners."

"*Your* partners?"

"I'm sure you wouldn't have heard since you pulled back from the table and your head is so far up your ass, but since Caesar died, I'm in charge now. We know about your little alliance with Shamar. That shit just don't sit well with me. And on top of that, I don't even know if your hands are one hundred percent clean in my uncle's death."

"So, I guess this is the part where y'all kill me, you get the glory, and business continues as usual?"

"Nah, this is the part where we snatch you up, torture you for days, and then we kill you. Might be a little glory after that, but I'm in it more for the satisfaction of watchin' you die."

Boogie was growing impatient. He had to admit that Nicky had balls showing up in Brooklyn like that. He was truly caught off his square, especially with the new information swarming through his mind. The only thing he wanted to do was get inside his vehicle and drive off, but Nicky was in the way of that.

"You know . . ." Boogie's voice drifted for a second as he eyed Nicky curiously. "When I pulled up on Li, he was surrounded by his shooters. I killed them first. Then I handled him. I was wonderin' for a second if you killed mine and that's why you felt bold enough to show your face around here. But that dot on your man's head tells me that my snipers are about to let off on y'all."

Boogie looked at the man standing closest to Nicky and smirked. Nicky whipped around just in time to witness the red dot on his man's head before it exploded.

The sniper's bullet was swift and powerful; the gunshot was silent. Shortly after that man fell to the ground with half of his face missing, the others began dropping like flies too. They started firing wild shots into the sky, not knowing what buildings the snipers were on.

Nicky's focus, however, was still on Boogie. He ducked and shot relentlessly at him as Boogie hopped in his vehicle. He emptied his full clip, but there was no point. The Lamborghini was armored.

"Fall back!" Boogie heard Nicky shouting as he sped away.

He checked his rearview mirror just in case they decided to hawk him down, but they didn't. When they pulled out of the parking lot, they drove the other way. Boogie's heart was racing. He had kept it player in front of Nicky, but that was a close one. Had he pulled up on Nicky anywhere else rather than in front of his own businesses, it would have been a wrap for him. Boogie made a mental note to keep security detail around him at all times. He'd been so used to only moving with two to four people around him for years on heists, but he had to remind himself that things were different now. He was a walking target.

He kept checking his rear to make sure nobody was following him until he reached his destination. He parked in the roundabout driveway outside of his family home. He saw his mother's BMW and her two Mercedes, but he didn't see the Jeep anywhere, and that let him know she wasn't home. Even if she was, he didn't know what he was going to say to her.

As he walked to the front door, he pulled out his house key. However, when he tried it in the lock, it wouldn't turn. It took only a split second to register that the locks had been changed. It wasn't uncommon for the locks on the house to be swapped out with new ones, but they'd just been changed a few weeks ago. Also, technically speaking, it was his house. He was usually notified and provided with new keys. He checked under a potted plant to see if the spare was there. It wasn't. He gritted his teeth and had just turned to take the walk back to his car when the door opened.

"Bryshon! It's so nice to see you!"

Boogie whipped back around to see Marisol, one of the family's longtime housekeepers. There was something different about her that he couldn't put his finger on. She was Latina and black, with hair white as snow braided down her back. She was a petite little thing, but if Boogie remembered right, she had a bark that could put down even the biggest of dogs. She was the only person in his life that didn't address him by his nickname. In her old age, she had dropped down to part time and was rarely ever at the Tolliver residence when Boogie was, but he was happy that she was there now.

"Marisol," Boogie said fondly and gave her a hug.

"I thought that was you. You are just as handsome as you'll ever be!" she exclaimed, kissing his cheeks before ushering him in the house. "Your mother had these damn locks changed yesterday."

"I kind of figured somethin' was up when my key wouldn't turn," Boogie said, hiding his smirk.

"And still as sarcastic as ever. You better do good and remember I was never afraid to pop you in your mouth," she warned, and he knew better than to test her.

"Is Ma home?" Boogie asked, closing the front door behind him.

"No, and thank God she isn't. Your mother is driving me crazy! I'm thinking about coming back full time because she lets this house get so bad! Your father would turn over in his grave if he saw what I've seen."

"Maybe she's still mourning."

"Hmph." Marisol made a face. Boogie caught it and wondered what that was about. "Come. I'll make you something to eat."

She tried to take his elbow, but he shook his head. He had come there in search of answers, not to eat her famous grilled ham and cheese sandwich, even though it was one of his favorites.

"I'm sorry, Mari. I didn't come here to eat. I came here lookin' for . . ." He realized he didn't even know what he was looking for specifically.

"Looking for what, son?"

"I guess I'm lookin' for answers."

"About your father?" she asked.

He shook his head slowly, and her face grew intrigued. "About your mother?"

"Yes."

"Well then, baby, a grilled ham and cheese sandwich is just what you need. Come." She patted Boogie on the back, encouraging him to follow her.

He sighed and gave in. Maybe he could think more clearly with some food in his gut. He sat at the porcelain island and watched her bustle around the kitchen. When she was done grilling the sandwich in the pan, she cut off the crust and put potato chips in the center of it. When she placed it in front of him, the first thing he did was mash it down, making her laugh.

"You haven't changed one bit! I remember when you were a boy and had to start spending your Sundays with me. All you would talk about was how Diana would make your sandwiches, and how I couldn't do it right. But eventually, you liked mine too."

She took some juice out of the fridge so she could pour him a tall glass. When she brought it to him, she sat on the stool beside him and watched him eat. He glanced at her and finally realized why she looked different.

"When did you start wearin' a uniform?" he asked, nodding at the blue maid's outfit she wore.

"Ever since your mom told me last week I had to, or else I wouldn't have a job. If I didn't have grandkids, I would have said screw her! I'm almost seventy years old. I should be able to come to work comfortable."

"You should have just come to me. I would have sorted it out."

"Always my sweet boy," she said and touched his face tenderly. "So, what is it that you want to know? And be sure to ask the right questions."

Boogie took one more bite of his food before washing it down with the fruit punch she'd brought to him. There was something about the way she spoke that made him believe she knew something. He pushed the food away and turned to look into her awaiting face.

"I want to know . . . I want to know if my father ever cheated on my mother with Diana."

"I never saw your father with Miss Diana, but I do know he cared deeply for her, the way a man would for a woman he loves. He made her your godmother, you know."

"I remember," Boogie said honestly.

Whereas he never knew that Caesar was his godfather, he remembered Diana. Vividly. His happiest moments as a child had been with her. As an adult, they were thoughts he pushed to the side, because as he got older, the love he had for her turned to anger. She had never tried to see him again after the day his mother snatched him away from her house. That shouldn't have been enough to keep her away. Soon, that anger diminished, and any feeling he had toward her faded, or so he thought.

"Do you think my mama had proof that they were a thing?"

"Why do you ask?"

"Because I want to know if she ever had a reason to cheat back," he said, and Marisol gave a small smile.

"Now, that is the right question."

"Did she?"

Marisol sighed and looked around the house as if Dina would pop up any second. When she turned back to him, she leaned forward and spoke in a low voice.

"You never saw your mother the way I did . . . the way your father did. She was a good mother to you, or at least she tried to be, but . . ."

"But what?"

"The real her, the unmedicated her, is irrational."

"Unmedicated?"

"Yes. She could be a very mean woman at times. If it weren't for your father begging me to stay and me knowing you needed me, I would have quit a long time ago. I stayed after your father's passing because I'd dropped to part time, and I wouldn't have to deal with your mother's episodes as much."

"What are you tryna tell me, Mari?"

"I . . ." she started, and then paused. She looked at him deeply in his eyes, and he found sadness in hers. "In the back of her closet, there is a wooden box. Open it. The answers you seek are in there."

She gave his hand two pats before getting up from the stool and heading to tend to her duties. Somehow, Boogie felt more confused than he had when he first sat down. He decided to go see what she was talking about.

He headed upstairs to the bedroom his parents had once shared. When he got there, he wasn't prepared to be taken aback the way that he was. The room had been completely refurnished, and any remnant of Barry had been wiped clean away. There were no pictures on the walls, and the mahogany California king–size bed had been replaced with a canopy bed. There was a vanity in the corner where his father's reading chair had been. The room he remembered was no more.

He collected himself and went to the closet. Before he opened the door, he figured Barry's clothes had been removed too, but seeing them actually gone was something else.

Boogie did as Marisol said and went to the back of the large closet. The wall to the left was filled completely with shoes, and the wall to the right was color coordinated with all of his mother's clothes. There was a large full-size mirror attached to the wall in the back, and a diamond-studded ottoman sat in front of it. Next to the mirror, attached to the same wall, were eye-level shelves. On the top one was a small handcrafted wooden box with designs carved into it. He looked over his shoulder before grabbing it.

Never in his life had Boogie gone through his mother's things, and he felt like he was breaking some sort of code. Still, he sat down on the ottoman and opened the box without hesitation. It was filled with many things, but a bottle of pills was on top.

"Olanzapine." He read the bottle's label out loud. "'Take ten milligrams a day to help with symptoms caused by bipolar disorder.'"

Bipolar disorder? His mother was bipolar? If she was, he'd had no ide—

He suddenly thought back to the day Dina had come to snatch him from Diana's house. He had never seen her so angry before. She was rough with him, and the whole way home, she cursed him out. She never cursed at him. He wondered if that was the cause of her behavior that day.

Setting the pill bottle aside, he continued digging through the box until he came across some Polaroid pictures. The first few were of her in the bed, wrapped in a cover. He couldn't see anything but her bare shoulders and knew she was naked.

"Gross." His stomach lurched, thinking they were photos his father had taken when he was alive.

He was just about to put the photos back and close the box when he came to the next photo in the bunch. It made his skin crawl and sent an uneasy feeling to his gut. It was another photo of his mother in bed with someone, but the person wasn't his father. It was Julius. He was kissing her neck in a way that a man shouldn't kiss his right-hand man's lady. The next photo was of his mother doing a sexual activity to Julius that made him throw the photos back inside the box. He wanted to burn what he had just seen from his memory. Dina had cheated on his father with Julius?

The way he had found her in Julius's office earlier that day made sense now. He thought about how tenderly she'd been caressing the desk. She was reminiscing about her lover. But what did it all mean?

He closed the box and placed it where he'd found it. As he was about to exit the closet, his attention was caught by a pile of clothes in the far corner. They were sitting outside of a hamper, like someone had started to do laundry but stopped and had just forgotten about them. Poking out from the middle of the pile was the pants leg of what looked like a sweat suit. It looked like the same one he'd seen Dina wearing the night she came to his house.

He kicked the clothes around it to the side and saw that the pants were balled up with the jacket. His eyes went from the pants to the jacket, and then to the white tank top still inside the jacket. It was like Dina had come home and snatched off everything. The red droplets on the white shirt stood out like stripes on a zebra. Blood. It was blood. He hadn't noticed it that night, or maybe he had and just didn't remember. Too many emotions were coursing through him at that time. But right then, the blood stared back at him, plain as day.

He went to pick up the shirt to get a closer look, but he heard voices outside of the closet. Someone had come into the room.

"Ma'am, I can tell you've had a long day. Come down and eat. I'll turn on something for you to watch," Marisol was saying quickly.

Her tone had a pleading quality, and Boogie felt that it was because she figured he was still somewhere in the room. He tiptoed to the closet door and peeked out. Marisol was trying to grab her arm and take her back out of the room, but Dina snatched away.

"Um, this is a full-grain leather jacket. Get your hands off of it! Just leave me the hell alone, Marisol," Dina snapped. "You just followed me all the way to my room, and you see I'm on the phone. I'll be down when I feel like it."

"But ma'am—"

"Woman, if you don't leave me the hell alone, I'm going to see to it that you never see those grandchildren of yours again! If you want to make yourself useful, pull my car to the front. I had to take the back road to the house today."

"Yes, ma'am," Marisol said and glanced quickly in the direction where Boogie was hiding.

She left the room, and Boogie went to the back of the closet again. Dina parking in the back of the house was the only reason she didn't know her son was there, and he hoped he could keep it that way. He hid behind a rack of Dina's long furs and hoped she didn't come in the closet.

She moved around in the bedroom, and he heard her talking on the phone. He was trying to think of the best way to get out of the situation he was in. The only thing that was in the closet was a laundry chute. He might have been able to fit inside it when he was a boy, but he probably couldn't even fit both his shoulders through anymore. He continued wracking his brain until he heard her address the person on the phone.

"Shamar, your men will live. You act like they've never taken a beating before. Boogie is just on a power trip, that's all."

Boogie heard movement near the closet's entrance and tensed up, thinking she was about to come inside. However, all she did was throw a pair of boots inside. One of them nearly hit him, but he stayed still.

"No, I don't think he suspects a thing. Don't be ridiculous. He's just as clueless as his father was," she continued, and then paused. "Don't be so hasty. I told you not to make any moves from the inside until I get him to add me as part owner to all of the businesses! So, when he's out of the way, it will all come to me. That was our deal!" Pause. "Well, if you're going to do that, at least wait for me to handle what I need to before then. I won't let another man be a snake in my bed. I'll be damned if he leaves me with nothing too! That's where Julius fucked up at when he killed Barry. He was supposed to wait. So now I hope you do the job right." Pause. "Boogie listens to everything I say. I'm the one who put the idea of this silly war in his head to begin with, remember? Soon he'll be out of the way, and I'll finally be free of Tolliver men!"

That time, the pause was longer. She moved around all around the room, and Boogie heard the sound of drawers opening and closing.

"What do you mean how much time do I need? The question is, how much time do *you* need? I thought you needed Boogie to take out the other families so you can take control over the drug trade. You're welcome again for Caesar, by the way." Pause. "You don't need Boogie anymore? Well, look at you being sneaky with something under your sleeve. If that's the case, we might as well turn two jobs into just one. I'll let you know when and where we will be." She disconnected the phone.

Boogie couldn't believe what he had just heard. From her own mouth, his mother said that she and Julius had conspired to kill Barry. He thought back to the tears she cried and how distraught she had seemed when news of Barry's passing first came to light. It had all been an act, a very convincing one, too. Boogie had never suspected a thing.

He didn't even care to wonder how she and Shamar had gotten so close. As conniving as she was, there was no telling. It took all his willpower not to burst out from the closet and strangle her. How could she do this?

The sound of water running interrupted his thoughts. Dina had turned on the shower, and when he heard her singing a sweet tune from the bathroom, he snuck out and made a beeline for the door. He had the sickest feeling coursing through his veins. He had been nothing but a puppet to both Dina and Shamar. All he could think about was how badly he had messed up.

Chapter 16

If it weren't for the thick black mink fur coat she wore that matched the over-the-knee boots on her feet, Diana might have felt the cold air circling around her. She was sitting outside of her condo in Harlem as she oversaw the activities of her girls along the streets. A self-care book rested in her lap, and she flipped through the pages with her gloved fingers.

It had been two days since she left the safety her fortress had to offer, and Diana couldn't remember the last time she was wary to move around New York. The car chase had taken a toll on her, more than she cared to admit. She might have still looked fabulous, but the facts were the facts. She wasn't young anymore. She thought she would be able to withstand the war in the field, but after all of that, she didn't know. It was apparent that Boogie would do whatever, wherever, and she feared that, not for just herself, but for everything she'd built. She had grown too attached to the things around her and began wondering if continuing to fight was the best course of action. Even Nicky had tried to go at Boogie and failed.

She sighed and continued trying to read her book until a resolve found her.

"How to truly remain calm under stress." Morgan's voice sounded, coming up from beside of her.

She too was bundled up in a fur and had a thick Russian fox hat over the top of her head. The tall heels she wore made Diana realize she was losing her touch. She hadn't even heard the girl coming.

"You know it's rude to read over someone's shoulder?" Diana closed her book and scooted over so Morgan could take a seat.

"I'm sorry. I just got bored being in there by myself." She sighed as she plopped down. "I'm so tired of watching TV, and if I keep eating like this, I'm going to be as big as a house!"

"Trust me, that figure you have should be good for a lot more years," Diana assured her.

"When am I gonna be able to go back to work?" Morgan pouted. "The club is probably going to shit without us there."

"Things at the club are fine. It's only been a few days. We will go when there isn't a target on my back."

"And when is that gonna be?"

"I don't know," Diana told her. "But you're in this now because of me. I don't want anything to happen to you. We are safe here."

"Ugh!" Morgan groaned, making Diana chuckle.

"You need to learn patience if you expect me to ever teach you how to shoot a gun."

Diana's phone began to vibrate in her bag, and she took it out, thinking it was one of her girls, but she didn't recognize the number on the screen. She answered, it and placed it to her ear.

"This is Diana."

"If I drive down this street, tell your snipers not to shoot. I'm in a black Lamborghini."

It was Boogie. Her smile washed away immediately, and she got a sour taste in her mouth.

"You have some nerve still calling this phone."

"Are you gon' tell them or not?"

"And why on earth would I do that after all you've done? You killed one of my girls and just tried to kill me."

"Your girl just got caught in the crossfire. That was never meant to happen. And as far as what happened to you, that . . . that wasn't me. Shamar's shooters acted alone, without my say so. I swear."

He sounded sincere, but Diana still didn't trust him.

"Aren't you the one that brought them here?"

"Yeah, but—"

"Then you are just as responsible as they are."

"Diana, please. I need to talk to you. Shit is fucked up right now. I don't know where else to go."

She didn't just hear the need in his voice; she felt it. She inhaled a brisk breath, trying to make a decision. If she let him through, he could very well kill her and Morgan. It could all be a trap.

"You promised me when I was little that you would always be there for me. Well, I need you right now. Please, Diana. I'm alone."

She squeezed the phone tight and pulled it away from her face. Her finger disconnected the call, and she stared at the device. In that moment, she hated herself for making that promise to him all those years ago. Now she was put in the position to keep it. She made a call to her cousin Christian way down the block.

"Hello?"

"There is a black Lamborghini that is about to drive down the street. Let him through."

"But isn't that—"

"Let him through."

"Yes, ma'am."

She hung up and put the phone back in her purse. When she looked up again, Morgan was looking at her as if she had just lost her mind.

"Didn't you just tell me how you didn't want anything to happen to us? Now you're letting this crazy mother-fucka just waltz over here?"

"Something about him seemed . . . different. Plus, I have snipers on every roof for half a mile. If he tries anything, he will die where he stands."

"I hope you're right about this."

Diana did too. Shortly after she disconnected with Christian, the Lamborghini came creeping up the block. It slowed to a stop in front of the bench they were sitting on, and Boogie stepped out. Although he wore a fitted suit with a nice dress coat over it, his face looked like he hadn't slept in days. He came and stood in front of them and put his hands in his pockets.

"I'll grant you five minutes of my time, so make it count. What do you want?" Diana snapped.

"I know who killed Caesar."

Diana felt herself rise in her seat. That was one hell of a way to start a conversation. She handed the book to Morgan and stood up. Morgan grabbed her wrist to prevent her from getting any closer to Boogie, but Diana signaled that it was okay. Morgan let her go and glared at Boogie, daring him silently to do something stupid.

"And how did you come across this knowledge?" she inquired.

"I heard the person admit it."

"Mmm, and I'm assuming this information comes with a cost."

"It does," he admitted.

"And that would be?"

"For you to help me kill them and everybody else involved."

"And why would you want to do that?"

"Because the person is also responsible for what happened to my father," Boogie said and probed her eyes with his. "It was my mother."

"Dina?" Diana asked in disbelief.

"Yeah," Boogie said. "I heard her admitting to it on the phone when I was hidin' in her closet."

"But why would she do something so heinous? Barry was her husband!"

"She was havin' an affair with Julius. I think she was just tryna get my pops out of the way so they wouldn't have to be in the dark anymore. I think Caesar found out about what really happened and killed Julius. And then my mom killed him."

"The person in the black sweat suit . . ."

"That was her. She came over my house wearing it, and I put two and two together when I saw it in her closet with Caesar's blood."

"Holy shit." Diana breathed raggedly. "Holy fucking shit!"

"I fucked up, Diana. I fucked up bad." Boogie put his head in his hands, and out of instinct, Diana wrapped her arms around him.

"She manipulated you, Boogie. She used your emotions to her advantage."

"But the Chinese . . ."

"We'll cross that road when we come to it." She rubbed his back in a comforting motion and tried to soak up his grief. She couldn't imagine all that he was feeling. A mother was supposed to love and protect their children, not use them to her personal gain.

When Boogie regained his composure, he stood straight again. Diana's heart broke at the pain in his eyes, and any bad feeling she had about him washed away. Just like that.

"She and Shamar are plottin' to kill me, and then they're gon' go for the rest of you. He was just usin' me to weaken the families."

"Well, I'm glad you figured out what they were up to before that could happen."

"Are y'all just gonna skip over the part where he said he was hiding in her closet?"

Both Boogie and Diana turned their heads to Morgan, who was still sitting on the bench. Diana couldn't lie; with all that Boogie had just told her, she forgot the girl was right there.

"Who are you?" Boogie asked.

"The person whose gonna fuck you up if you're lying to us," Morgan told him.

"I'm not."

"I believe him," Diana said, and took him by the arm. "Come inside. It's cold out here."

"Hmm," Morgan said under her breath and stood to her feet.

The three of them ventured into Diana's condo. The inside was much nicer than the outside. At one point, it had been two apartments, but when she needed a low place to live, she turned it into one living space.

She made Morgan and Boogie sit at the glass table in her dining room area until she was done making them some tea.

"How did you find me?" she asked Boogie when she placed a teacup on a coaster in front of him.

"I figured you weren't gon' be at your house, so I drove through Harlem in one of my other cars until I found the place with Dominicans standing out front."

"Smart," Diana commented, sitting across from them.

"Sounds a little stalkerish to me," Morgan said before taking a sip of her drink.

"I had to do what I had to do. Shamar is plannin' on makin' a move on me by the end of the week. And with all this shit goin' on underneath my nose, I don't think it would be smart to underestimate either one of them."

"I agree. We need a plan," Diana said.

"I can bring the Italians into the fold," Boogie suggested.

"The Italians?" Diana asked, raising a brow.

"Aw, yeah. I took over their spot when Bosco died," Boogie said sheepishly.

"And does Shamar know that?"

"Yup."

"So there won't be any surprise there then," Diana said.

"Nah, but I'm supposed to meet my mo—Dina on Friday. She thinks I'm gon' make her partial owner of the businesses."

"Where does she want to meet you?"

"At this Italian spot in Staten Island," Boogie said, and Diana gazed at him over her teacup.

"That's when it's going to happen then," she said.

"When what's gonna happen?" he asked her.

"When they're going to try and kill you. So make sure you go."

"What?"

"If it's in Staten Island, you have an advantage. However, they're expecting you to be unsuspecting. They think you're going to walk in clueless. You'll be busy signing papers, and the next thing you know, you have a bullet in your head in front of all of your people because Shamar sniped you. And then he takes over where you left off."

"How do you know all of that?"

"Because it's what I would do. There is no better prey than a sitting duck. But good for you, you won't be that. You're going to play your role until we can snuff Shamar out. And when we're done with him, we—no, *I* handle that bitch of a mother of yours."

Ring! Ring!

A phone ringing loudly from the living room got their attention. The sound of it made Diana's heart skip a beat. Could it be?

"You have a house phone?" Morgan asked humorously.

"Yeah, what is this. The nineties?" Boogie added.

"Yeah, I do have a house phone, but it never rings," Diana said, getting to her feet.

She walked quickly to answer it. There was only one person in the world who had that phone number, because only one person knew where to find her if she wasn't at home or at the club. She looked over her shoulder to make sure Morgan and Boogie weren't paying her any attention. They weren't. They were too busy taking digs at each other's outfits.

"Hello?" she whispered.

"If I had to call one more number to get a hold of you, I was just going to come find you myself."

The voice brought a smile to her face, and she let out a happy breath. "Caesar. You're awake."

Chapter 17

"You look like shit."

Those were the first words Caesar spoke when he saw her. She had never been so happy to be insulted in her life. He was a sight for sore eyes when she entered the bedroom as he was trying to down some applesauce. He wore a long-sleeve silk pajama set, and the hair on his head and his face had grown out. A shave would do him more than some good. His deep voice was a little raspy from not being used for so long, and he'd lost a few pounds, but he was still Caesar.

"I could say the same about you." She grinned and took a seat beside the bed.

"Well, I have a reason to look terrible. I was shot. What's your excuse?"

"Life." She shrugged. "Are you sure you should be sitting up like that?"

"I've been laying down for weeks. My back needs some stretch."

"Well, at least let me make you comfortable. What do you have an in-home nurse for if she's not doing her job?" Diana propped some pillows behind his back so that he could sit comfortably without using too much energy.

"In her defense, I haven't been the most pleasant person since returning to the land of the living," Caesar said and set the applesauce to the side. "I don't need two guesses on why I'm here in this house."

"We had to hide you until we knew who tried to kill you. The world thinks you're dead."

"I would have done the same if it were one of you in my position."

"I know you would have."

"I only called you when I woke up," he said with a serious tone. "I needed to tell you that I know who tried to kill me."

"It was Dina. I know already."

"How?" he asked with a curious expression on his face.

"So much has happened since you've been gone." Diana sighed. "But Boogie was the one who figured it out and told me."

"He was so angry with me the last time I saw him," Caesar said sadly. "How is he?"

"He went on a rampage when he thought you were the one who killed Barry, and Li is dead because of it," she told him. "Dina used his anger and his pain against him. She manipulated him. Now, after all that he's done, he needs my help, because his own pet snake is about to bite him in the ass."

She continued telling him everything that had transpired, from Shamar being in New York to the plot on Boogie's life. When she was done talking, she expected him to say something, anything, but Caesar was quiet. It was a deafening silence, and Diana wondered if she should have kept it all to herself.

"Sounds to me like you have a big decision to make," was all Caesar said when he finally spoke.

"That's it? After everything I just told you, that's what you have to say? Did you even hear me when I said that he killed Li?"

"Yes, I heard you. I don't know if it's the pain medication or what, but when you said that, all I could think about is I'm glad it wasn't you or Marco. And that alone leads me to wonder if his actions with that are truly unforgivable."

"He's done so much and made so many enemies in such a short time. I just don't know how I can help him. How does a person come back from that?"

"The same way you did," he told her simply.

She wanted to avert her gaze from the knowing look he was giving her. Not wanting to agree, she shook her head in denial. There was no comparison between her and Boogie.

"What I did was an accident." The tone of her voice was low and shaky. "I was only eighteen. I didn't mean for my father to die that night. How was I supposed to know the pizza man I let in the house was really a hit man? I still have the visual in my head of my papá lying with his throat slit. It took a long time for me to forgive myself for that."

"And what about the rest of your family? Did they forgive you?"

"Not at first. For a while, they thought I'd orchestrated the whole thing to take his place, but I *still* would trade all of this for one day with my papá. But eventually, yes, they did forgive and accept me. With the help of you, of course. You told them that I was young and only human, and that there were still many teachable moments ahead of me."

"Then the same will be said for Boogie," Caesar said simply.

"I don't think all will welcome Boogie back to the fold with open arms."

"New York is only as strong as its weakest link, and right now, it's Boogie. He unknowingly has gotten into bed with the devil. There was once a time when I would have ordered his death without a second thought. But out of everything you told me, the only thing that really matters to me right now is that he's seen the truth and wants to right the wrongs he can. When the time comes, you let me worry about Nicky and the rest of my family," Caesar said. "Right now, he's probably under the pressure of living up to me."

"Not for much longer. Just until you recover and come back," Diana reminded him, but she noticed the solemn expression on Caesar's face. "What?"

"Since I woke up from my coma, I've been thinking."

"About?"

"I think what the game needs is fresh blood. We had a good run under the pact, but all things come to an end. What if the tragedy behind Barry's death was the beginning of something beautiful? I mean, I can't help but to think that maybe it's been past the time to pass the torch. We've just been so stubborn, and now our hands are being forced."

"You could walk away from it all? Just like that?"

"I'm old, but still young enough to step away from the throne and live my remaining days the way I see fit. Being on the brink of death taught me that I haven't done anything I really want to do in a long time."

She studied him and could find sincerity on every corner of his face. He was really ready to retire. Diana didn't know why, but the thought of retiring made her nervous. There was still so much to do, and she didn't trust anyone to do it. Still, she was on the same page as him. She was older, but still young enough to enjoy the rest of her life.

For as long as she could remember, she had been a part of the game. Her life was pretty much chosen for her. She never even thought about doing or being anything, so a part of her would rather spend her last years doing and being something else.

"I understand." She grabbed his hand, giving it a squeeze. "More than you know. Whatever you decide, I'm behind you. But before I even think about that, I have to sort this shit out with Boogie. He's meeting with Dina on Friday. She wants him to make her part owner to everything Barry built."

"As soon as he does that, she's going to have him killed."

"My thoughts exactly."

"I never did like her," Caesar noted. "Barry would have done much better by choosing you. She might not have killed him with her hands, but she is very much responsible. And now she's trying to do away with his legacy. Her own son. Diana, you'll have to kill them first. Every last one of them who poses a threat. Otherwise—"

"I'm not going to let them kill our godson."

There was a wave of something that went throughout the room. Diana couldn't quite place it, but it was felt. Caesar squeezed her hand fondly and nodded. He opened his mouth to say something else, but the only thing that came out were a fit of coughs. His body jerked, and he was forced to let her hand go.

The nurse came rushing in the room to tend to him. Diana watched her help him lie back down and check his vitals. When he stopped coughing, she wagged her finger at him.

"Mr. King, it's a miracle that you're awake after all that your body went through, but if you plan on making a full recovery, then you have to preserve your strength." The nurse turned to Diana and gave her an apologetic look. "I think maybe he needs to get some more rest. You're more than welcome to stay or come back another time."

"I'll be back tomorrow," she said, but Caesar shook his head.

"No. I don't want to see you until you take care of what you need to. I'm not going anywhere."

She smiled and stood from the chair. Her lips found his forehead, and she bid him farewell.

She left and headed back to the condo where Morgan was waiting for her. With Caesar awake, that was one less thing for her to worry about. Yet somehow, the load she carried didn't seem any lighter.

Chapter 18

Since Boogie was on a path of righting wrongs, he had another stop to make. He didn't know what the future had in store for him, but he knew what was in his heart. He hadn't seen or talked to Roz since the day she stormed out of his condo, but she had been on his mind. She was a rare woman, and even if she didn't take him back, he wanted her to know that.

He honestly didn't remember driving to her house, but somehow, he ended up there. The blinds were open partially, and he stood in front of the window, watching her in the living room. She was sitting on the couch and tickling Amber's toes. Those smiles. He had missed them.

The thought that maybe they would be better off without him crossed his mind as he continued to watch. But then again, the thought of another man being in their lives made him sick. He loved them. He never thought that he would have a "person" until he met Roz. She was his person, and he wasn't ready to lose that.

Boogie took his phone out of his pocket and scrolled down to where it said WIFEY with a heart. He hit the call button and placed the phone to his ear. He watched her phone light up on the arm of the couch. He also saw her look at it, and when she saw it was him, a small smile found her lips. However, when she answered the phone, attitude dripped from her voice.

"I thought I told you don't call me."

"Is that what you said? I don't remember."

"It was somethin' like that. What do you want?" She leaned back into the couch.

"Do you still love me?" Boogie asked.

"You can't answer my question with a question. Conversations don't work like that."

"Well, that's what I want. To know if you still love me."

"Boogie . . ."

"It's a simple yes or no answer."

"Boy, you know I still love your ass. What the fuck kind of stupid question is that?" she asked, and he laughed.

"Well, shit, I don't know, with how easy it was for you to quit me."

"Maybe . . . maybe I was wrong for that."

"Whaaat?" Boogie feigned shock. "Say that again. I don't think I heard you right, shorty."

"Maybe I was wrong." Roz groaned. "My brother just made me realize some shit. No, I don't like the thought of you puttin' yourself in danger every day, or the shit you've been up to. But he was right when he said I knew the kind of nigga you were when I got with you. Just like you knew I had baggage before you got with me, and you never judged me."

"I would never look at Amber as baggage, because she's an extension of you," Boogie told her earnestly. "I accept every piece of you because you make me feel things nobody else ever has. I love you."

"I love you too. So, does this mean you're comin' home?"

"I have some loose ends to tie up. I wish I would have listened to you from the jump."

"Is everything okay?"

"It will be once I handle some business."

"Well, just be careful. Amber doesn't have time for anything to happen to her daddy—"

The moment the words were out of her mouth, she knew she couldn't take them back. Boogie watched as her hand went to her mouth, as if she couldn't believe she had just said them. Her eyes closed, and when Boogie didn't say anything due to his own personal shock, she cleared her throat.

"My bad. I didn't mean—"

"I can be that." Boogie cut her off. "I mean, I'm probably gon' marry her annoyin'-ass mama one day anyway, so that's fine."

"Her mama is not annoyin'!" She laughed. "She's the best thing that ever happened to you."

"You might be right about that." Boogie paused and just stared at her fondly. He wanted more than anything to go inside and be with them, but he knew if he did that, he wouldn't want to leave. "I love you, Roz."

"I love you too. Whatever it is that you gotta do, please just be careful."

"No doubt."

He disconnected the phone and turned his back on the house. He'd shown up under the pretense of making things right just in case something happened to him. But when he left, he told himself that nothing *would* happen to him. He made a silent promise to himself that he would make it back to them.

It was early in the day Friday, and he still had a lot to do before he met up with Dina that evening. In his mind, he had stopped referring to her as his mother, just as she couldn't have referred to him as her son.

The first stop he had to make was to meet Bentley and Gino. They were awaiting his arrival at a warehouse dock they used to traffic stolen goods in and out with regular household products. It had been one of his father's smartest ideas. It was Friday, so of course it was busy, and when Boogie got there, everyone he walked by acknowledged their boss. He found Bentley and Gino at the furthest end of the dock by the water. To his surprise, Tazz was there too, and he didn't look happy.

"So, you weren't gon' let me in on this little soiree you have goin' on later?" Tazz said as Boogie approached and stood in front of them.

"I just didn't wanna get too many people involved," Boogie told him. "We're all in this shit because I was too stupid to see what was really what."

"We're family, though. We ride together no matter what. If we die together, we just die together."

"Bad boys for life," Gino spoke up, and Tazz narrowed his eyes at him. "What? I just thought it was a good time to throw that in."

"A'ight, enough with the sentimental shit. Let's get down to business," Boogie said and looked at Bentley. "Did you get what Diana asked for?"

"You know it." Bentley nodded and took a wire and three earpieces from his pocket. "When you put this under the shirt you're gon' wear tonight, Diana and I will be able to hear anything you say and everything that's said to you."

"I think maybe we should come up with a code word, just in case somethin' goes wrong," Tazz suggested.

"Yeah, somethin' like *gravy*!" Gino threw in.

"The fuck?" Tazz looked at him like he was stupid. "Yo, whose mans is this? Is he slow?"

"Let's go for somethin' more subtle, like *water*," Bentley said.

"A'ight, that's straight. Did you get that other thing I was lookin' for?" Boogie asked.

"Yeah, I downloaded it on my phone. Gather around, folks," Bentley said and pulled his phone out and held it up for them to see. On the screen was a blueprint of the restaurant Boogie was supposed to meet Dina in.

"A'ight," Bentley explained, "so Shamar has already let it be known that his shooters don't mind operating in the public eye, so we have to be on the lookout for any and everything. I highlighted all of the entrances and exits, and the dining area doesn't have windows. So, if he does make a move tonight, he would have to come from one of these places. Diana will have all of those doors covered. Tazz, it just hit me that Dina knows your face. So instead of you bein' in the restaurant with Gino and Boogie, you'll be outside in the van with the earpiece."

"Where are me and you gon' be at in the restaurant?" Gino asked.

"Dinin' somewhere close. It's supposed to be a simple dinner between mother and son. We don't want to alert her that we're on to her," Bentley answered.

"Gino, did you ever figure out where Shamar's shooters got their guns from?" Boogie asked.

"Nah, I just met dead end after dead end."

"Okay, well, let's just assume they're gon' have some heavy fire power. I'ma see you boys later. Keep your phones close and stay dangerous," Boogie said.

Boogie took the wire from Bentley and tucked it away in his pocket for later. The plan was solid, and he had a team ready to do whatever. Still, Boogie had a strange feeling in his stomach. He didn't know if it was from anticipation or because he knew something bad was going to happen either way the dice rolled.

Chapter 19

If Boogie had known how hard it was going to be for him to sit across a dinner table from Dina, he might have rethought the whole plan. Keeping it player was usually easy for him, but that evening, he had to keep reminding himself not to blow up the spot. He didn't want her to suspect him for anything. It was mind-blowing how well she played the loving mother role.

Bella e Buona was the restaurant name, and it was busy enough for Bentley and Gino to blend in with the crowd. Bentley also had an earpiece in, so although he wasn't in listening distance, he could hear everything that was going on.

Boogie and Dina sat toward the back at a square table in a reserved section away from most of the other patrons. There were a few Italian men enjoying a dinner not too far away from them, but other than that, they were alone. She sat there wearing a long-sleeved black Vera Wang dress with her hair pulled up into a neat bun to show off the diamonds in her ears. The red on her lips was fitting, since she was out for blood. Boogie didn't realize he was staring until she looked up and smiled at him.

"You look very handsome tonight in that suit," she told him. "I remember when your father used to take me to nice restaurants like this when we first started dating."

"Must seem like a lifetime ago now," Boogie said dryly.

"It does, but life must go on."

"I guess so."

An awkward silence fell over them before she cleared her throat and motioned toward his plate. "You've barely touched your spaghetti. You don't like it?" she asked. "If not, I can have them bring you something else. I want you to enjoy your meal."

Yeah, because you think it's my last one, huh? he found himself thinking but said something different.

"Nah, I'ma eat it. It's good."

"Are you sure? I can make them bring you some lasagna."

"I said it's good," Boogie snapped a little harder than he intended to.

"Yo, tone it down some, Boog. We don't want her thinkin' you're hostile," he heard Tazz say through the earpiece in his ear.

Tazz was right, but he couldn't help it. Hearing her talk about his father as if she wasn't the reason he was dead made him want to call her every name in the book. He tried to keep his thoughts from forming on his face, but something must have surfaced, because Dina gave him a concerned look.

"Are you all right, son? You seem a little tense."

"Yeah, I'm good," Boogie told her, calming himself down. "Work has just been weighin' me down. I feel like there's so much to do, and I only have one body."

"That's the cost of being a boss," she said and took a sip of red wine. "Speaking of being a boss, I do believe we're here for a reason?"

"We are, aren't we?"

Boogie pulled a folder from one of the seats on the side of the square table. He handed it to her and watched her open it and thumb through the files. The smile on her face started small and ended big.

"You signed all of them?" she asked.

"Yes, I did. Are you happy?"

"More than you even know," she said with a laugh.

"I'm sure you are."

It wasn't a regular laugh. It came off as a bit sinister. The loving eye she'd been giving him the whole dinner turned into a stare of disdain. She tucked the folder away in her oversized purse like she was afraid he would take it back, and she went back to eating her food.

Boogie glanced up and looked across the table at Bentley, who shook his head, letting him know no funny business was happening. Boogie didn't know what game Dina was trying to pull. He knew she had something up her sleeve ready to pop out like a Jack in the Box. When she was done eating, she finished the rest of her wine before excusing herself.

"I need to use the little girl's room. I'll be right back." She got up from the table and headed for the restrooms on the other side of Bella e Buona with her purse in tow.

"We're still all clear over here," Tazz said through the earpiece.

Boogie went back to eating his food. The restaurant actually made a good dish; however, he just didn't have much of an appetite when she was sitting across from him. When she came back to the table, he was almost finished. Since he didn't want to lose his appetite for a second time, he didn't look up at her. Big mistake.

"I see you like the food here." A man's voice sounded.

It was a familiar one to Boogie, and when he looked up, sure enough, it was Shamar. He was wearing a chef's uniform as a disguise and had a victorious look on his face. Boogie spit the food in his mouth back on the plate, causing Shamar to laugh.

"Don't worry. I didn't poison your food. What fun would that be," Shamar told him. "But I must say, the look on your face right now is priceless. Tell me. What's going through your head right now?"

No wonder why his people hadn't been able to spot Shamar. He was already inside. From the men's bathroom across the way, Boogie saw Major step out disguised as a bathroom attendant. He looked pissed, and Boogie figured it was because of the bruises that were all over his face.

He came and sat at the table next to Shamar and lifted his shirt, showing Boogie the submachine gun on his waist. The two of them must have been tucked away and waiting for their chance to strike. Boogie had to admit the tactic was cunning.

"I'm just thinking that I want some more water to wash down the nasty taste you're giving me," Boogie said.

"I bet you do. This game has been so exhilarating to play with you. You know the one where you thought that you were calling the shots and I played mouse. But that's over now," Shamar continued with a chortle. "A part of me wishes I would have let you cause a little more damage, but that's all right. The victory is sweet nonetheless. Almost as sweet as your mother's pussy. We've been plotting against you for a while now, and you fell right into Mommy's little trap. It's a shame that I'll have to do her in after I erase you from the map."

He searched Boogie's face for some sort of reaction but was met with none. Boogie was no longer surprised by anything Dina did. In fact, there was nothing that he would put past her. She was a woman searching for her own rise to power, and she was using what she had to get it.

"It's a lot of shit that has happened to me that I would've never seen comin'. Like you and my own mother conspiring against me. I'll let you know that I really thought I had you boxed in. So, I'll admit, when I found out that my mama was workin' with you to kill me, it was a shocker. But I bet you didn't expect me to have shooters ready and waitin' for you."

He motioned for Shamar to glance behind him. Both Bentley and Gino had heard the safe word and had sprung into action. Bentley stood by the table Major sat at with his hand in the jacket of his suit, daring him to move. He snatched Major's gun and tucked it on his hip. Gino was behind Shamar. He stood close and jabbed a gun to the back of his neck. The Italians at the nearby table kept glancing over to see what was going on, but Boogie just smiled and waved to let them know everything was fine.

The surprise on Shamar's face was priceless when he felt the cold steel on his neck. Boogie wished that he could just end him right then and there. Tazz had grown silent in his ear, and he figured he and Diana were making a move for the restaurant. By then, they should have heard what was going on.

A few moments later, Dina returned to the table from the restroom and had a look of confusion on her face.

"Have a seat, Mama," Boogie told her. "Or should I even call you that anymore?"

"I–I don't know what you're talking about, sweetheart," Dina said, looking from Bentley to Gino.

"Stop it with all the actin', yo," he demanded. "I know who and what you are—a psychotic bitch. And I said sit the fuck down!"

Dina eased slowly into a seat and whipped her head to face Shamar. "How could you let something like this happen? You were supposed to snatch him up when I was in the bathroom." Her voice was angry.

"You must have let something slip, because he knew what was going on," Shamar sneered. "I should have known not to trust a whore."

"Whore? Who are you calling a whore?"

"I believe he's talkin' to you," Gino answered, and she glared at him. "But I could be mistaken."

"Nah, he's right," Boogie confirmed. "Only a whore would do the things she's done."

"How dare you talk to your mother this way!"

"You ain't been my mama since you got my daddy killed," he said, and she pursed her lips.

"So you do know everything then," she said, leaning back into her seat. "Fine. I can finally be my real self with you. I never wanted you. If I didn't feel like your father was cheating on me, I would have never gotten pregnant to keep him. I knew he was going to be more successful than I could even imagine, but look how that turned out for me. He left everything to you, when *I'm* the one who helped build his empire. I'm the one who was there! Not you. I'm so glad he's dead."

"After killin' me, do you think this motherfucka would have let you just walk away?"

"Unlike you, I'm not so naïve. But I was going to cross that bridge when I got to it."

"There won't be any bridge to get to now. Gino, get that motherfucka up."

"Let's go," Gino said, jerking Shamar to his feet and pressing the pistol to his spine. "Who the fuck are you supposed to be anyways? Chef Boyardee?"

"Fuck you," Shamar replied.

"Before we take this walk outside and you die, I gotta know one thing. Who the fuck is Morty? The name on your weapons?"

Boogie didn't expect the loud laugh that came from Shamar's mouth. He then saw Major smirk. It was like the two of them were in on a joke that nobody else was included in.

"My plan hasn't changed. The only people who will be dying today are you," Shamar said, and his eyes found Boogie's. "And the name engraved on the guns isn't *Morty*. It's *Morte*. It's Italian for *death*."

On his last word, the Italian men sitting at the other table stood up. They whipped out guns from the waists of their suits and aimed toward Boogie. Behind Boogie, more Italians appeared, toting assault rifles.

The other people in the restaurant reacted in a frenzy and rushed to the exit, not wanting to have any part in what was going on. Boogie clenched his jaw as once again, the smug look returned to Shamar's face.

"Lower ya guns," an Italian voice barked behind Boogie.

Bentley and Gino looked around, ready to go out guns blazing, but when Boogie motioned for them to listen, they dropped their guns to their sides. The person who the voice belonged to walked around the table and stood beside Shamar. He was an older man who wore a black striped tailored suit and a fedora hat. The mustache above his lip was thick and gray, and his eyes were dark as night.

"Boogie, I don't think you've met Eduardo, Bosco's older brother."

Bentley and Boogie exchanged a look, mainly because neither of them knew Bosco had an older brother.

"See, when I told him about Bosco's untimely death, he wasn't sad at all. Bosco exiled him from his empire a long time ago. But now that he's dead, Eduardo here is interested in taking over where he left off. And, to be honest, the Italians in Staten Island would rather work under their own kind than the likes of you. As you can see." Shamar motioned to the men pointing guns at him.

"So, you made a deal with them the same as you made with me," Boogie said.

"A real businessman knows better than to take the first offer given to him. I had to look out for my best interest." Shamar shrugged. "They're willing to help me do whatever it takes to get what I want, including killing you and anyone else who stands in my way. What's that old saying? Ah, yes. Checkmate."

Chapter 20

A short time earlier

From a white van parked outside, the dinner seemed to be going off without a hitch to Diana. She and Morgan sat as Tazz listened to the conversation between Boogie and Dina. Diana understood that it must have been torture to sit there looking in her eyes, knowing all of the terrible things she had done, but he had to if their plan was going to work. Diana had her people standing near every door and monitoring everyone who came in and out of the restaurant. So far, Shamar was a no-show.

"What if he doesn't come?" Morgan said from the back, eating a bag of potato chips. "Then what?"

"Then we get Dina and use her to lead him to us," Tazz answered simply. "And can you stop crunchin' by my ear? I can't hear shit!"

"My bad. I eat when I'm nervous," Morgan admitted and put the chips away. "Why did you guys wear suits? I feel like I'm in a mobster movie right now and that I should've thrown on more than a hoodie and jeans."

"You'll learn," Diana told her simply and then turned her attention to Tazz. "What are they saying now?"

"Just makin' small talk really. I can tell Boog is gettin' irritated, though," Tazz said and then pressed a small button on his earpiece. "Yo, tone it down some, Boog. We don't want her thinkin' you're hostile."

"Can't she see the earpiece in his ear?" Morgan asked, looking at the one Tazz was wearing.

"Nah, the one he got is small enough to fit inside his ear cana. She shouldn't suspect a thing. And if she does, we'll hear it. Diana, can you check on our other boys?"

"Yes." Diana touched the button on the earpiece she had in her own ear. "Bentley, are you there?"

"I'm here."

"How are things looking on the inside?"

"Everything is everything on our end. Wait, Dina just got up to go to the bathroom."

"Okay, stay on high aler—"

"Shit!" she heard Boogie say into his mic.

"What's wrong?"

"Shamar just sat down at the table with Boogie."

"What? How? We didn't see him go in," Diana said as Tazz and Morgan focused their attention on her.

"He's wearin' a chef's uniform. This motherfucka is slick," Bentley said. "Should we move on him?"

"No," Diana told him. "Wait for him to give the code word."

"What's going on?" Morgan asked.

"Shamar is at the table with Boogie."

"What!" Tazz and Morgan exclaimed in unison.

"He dressed up as a chef. He probably snuck in right under our noses," Diana said, reaching for the glove compartment.

She pulled two Glock 19s from it and handed one to Tazz while she kept the other for herself.

"Hey, where's mine?" Morgan asked.

"You don't get one," Diana told her. "If anything happens, I want you to stay in the car where it's safe."

"That's not fai—"

"Code word!" Tazz said and looked at Diana. "Boogie just said the code word."

"Okay," Diana said and pressed the button on her earpiece. "Bentley. Boogie just said *water.*"

"A'ight, we're on it. I'm taking this out, but stand by."

Diana took her earpiece out and grabbed a walkie talkie from the arm rest of the van. All that was left to do was wait. Tazz still was listening through his earpiece with a smirk on his face.

"We got his ass," he said.

"What are you going to do to him?" Morgan asked.

"Killing men like Shamar right away is too easy," Diana told her. "I want him to suffer. Dina too. She will die the same way her husband did."

Without warning, Tazz's face dropped. He pushed the earpiece further into his ear as he tried to make out what was being said. Whatever it was had his eyes wide.

"What? What happened?" Diana asked.

"It's the Italians. They turned on us. We've got to get in there. Now!" Tazz threw the earpiece to the side and jumped out of the van.

Diana spoke into the walkie talkie. "Harley, if you can hear me, it's time to move. Get in there now!" Diana shouted and turned to see Morgan's fearful face. "I'll be back. Stay here!"

"Diana!" Morgan called, but she was already out of the van.

Parked behind the van was an all-black Escalade, and upon seeing Diana, the Dominicans inside filed out. As they rushed to the entrance of the restaurant, there was a flood of people running out in a panic. She weaved her way through them until she was inside.

In the near distance, she heard the loud bang of the first gunshots. She ducked down and gave her shooters the signal to go before her. They instantly took action, firing their weapons on the Italians and Shamar.

Diana checked the clip on her gun before she followed suit in a crouched down position. When finally she reached the action, she saw they were evenly numbered. Her men were dropping Italians, and the Italians were sending well-aimed bullets back. She saw Boogie dragging Tazz away from the gunfire. He was shot and was bleeding from the torso. Diana witnessed an Italian man aiming at them and shot him first. Her bullet hit him in the temple and snapped his neck to the side. Boogie was able to get Tazz safely out of the way for a moment and went back to the gunfight.

Saving them had given away her position, and an automatic weapon shot at her. She jumped out of the way just in time as the place she'd been standing was riddled with bullets. She spotted the shooter toting the AK out and fired her gun twice, catching him in the neck and the chest. She'd landed on her side hard when she jumped, and when she got to her feet, she stumbled a little.

"Somebody's getting old." She heard a voice and turned to see Dina standing behind her.

Diana tried to raise her gun, but Dina knocked it out of her hand. She then wrapped her long fingers around Diana's neck, forcing her into the wall behind her. Diana stared into her evil eyes as she was being suffocated. She tried to knee Dina, but the airtight grip she had on her neck wasn't letting up. Diana's fingers clawed at Dina's hands, and Dina gave a crazed laugh.

"I've wanted to do this for so long. You don't even know," Dina growled.

"Well, keep on waiting!" A voice sounded right before Dina was clocked hard in the head with something hard.

Dina released Diana's neck and dropped to the ground. Standing behind her was Morgan, holding a broken vase. Diana fell into her, catching her breath.

"I . . . thought I told you . . . to stay in the car," Diana said.

"I heard gunshots. I–I was worried."

"I had it under control," Diana lied, and Morgan gave her a look. "Okay, I was getting it under control. Stay back here, and this time, listen."

She made Morgan duck behind a large plant and removed a .22 from her ankle. She rejoined the fight, shooting and killing the nearest Italians to her. The rest seemed to know they had met their match and filed out while Gino and Bentley ran after them.

She needed to get to Boogie. He and Shamar were trading fire, but neither was seeming to hit their mark. Shamar's back was to Diana, and she pointed her weapon at the back of his kneecap before firing.

"Ahh!" He shouted in agony as he fell on his good knee.

"That's for all the bullshit you've caused," she said and hit the gun from his hand.

Boogie came from around the wall he'd been taking cover behind. Slowly he approached Shamar, who was trying to reach for a gun on his ankle. Boogie slapped him hard across the face with the butt of his gun, causing blood to spray from Shamar's mouth.

"And that's for tryna manipulate me," he said. "I should have killed you when I killed your son."

"Boogie!" Diana exclaimed. A dark-skinned man with locs crept up on him from behind, cocking his gun.

Bang! Bang! Bang! Bang!

Diana jumped, thinking Boogie had been hit, but to her surprise, it wasn't him who fell to the ground bleeding out. It was the man with the locs. His body twitched a few times from all the bullets in his back, but soon he was still. Behind him, Tazz had dragged himself to a wall and was sitting up. In his hand was a smoking pistol.

"Handle your business, cuz," Tazz said, breathing heavily.

"That was your last saving grace." Boogie leered down at Shamar. "You won't get another one. I was gon' take you and torture you, but—" *Bang!* Boogie cut himself off by shooting Shamar at point blank range, and the sound of his neck snapping seemed to echo. "I'm just gettin' tired of this game."

Diana rushed to tend to Tazz. She moved his hand out of the way to see the extent of the damage. There was a lot of blood, but it seemed to be a flesh wound. He would live.

Tazz smiled weakly when Boogie approached him. "My bad, cuz. I shouldn't have ran in here guns blazin' like that."

"Yeah, you really threw them Italian muthafuckas off by killin' their boss with your first bullet." Boogie glanced down at a dead Italian man wearing a striped suit.

"You know me. I always was good at makin' an entrance."

"How about we get you to make an entrance at a hospital. I don't need you dyin' on me," Boogie said.

"Diana!"

They were just about to help him up when Morgan screamed. Diana jumped to her feet and stared in horror when she saw Dina holding Morgan by the neck with a gun to her head. It was Diana's gun, the one she'd dropped. She could see the fear on Morgan's face.

"Drop your weapons or I'm going to kill this bitch!" Dina shrieked in a high-pitched voice.

"Do it!" Diana commanded before Boogie could make a move. "Just . . . do it."

When all of their guns were on the floor, Diana put her hands up and walked slowly toward Dina and Morgan.

"Stop moving," Dina shrieked again and pressed the butt of the Glock harder on Morgan's head.

"Okay. Okay. I'm stopped. Just let her go," Diana said, speaking calmly. "I'll give you whatever you want. Just let her go."

"Whatever I want?"

"Yes. Just name it and it's yours."

"I want your life!" Dina exclaimed, turning the gun to Diana and firing once.

Diana felt a fire in her side, followed by a pain she'd never experienced before. She staggered back and clutched the place where the bullet had entered. Her legs gave out on her, but before she could hit the ground, Boogie caught her.

"Diana!" His face was filled with concern.

"Don't follow me!" Dina shouted.

Diana's eyes shifted to her and saw that she was making a clean getaway with Morgan in tow. Diana tried to move but howled in pain. Her hands gripped Boogie's arm, and her eyes pleaded with him.

"Boogie . . ."

"Save your strength. I'm about to get help for both of you. Don't worry."

"No, Boogie, please. You have to get Morgan. Please!" she begged.

"I can't leave you."

"No, you have to save her!"

"Diana—"

"She's your sister!"

Her words put a pause on anything he was about to say. Diana felt herself losing consciousness, and the grip she had on his arm loosened.

"W–what?"

"Barry and I . . . we had a baby. He didn't know. I gave her up for adoption when she was born."

Diana couldn't hold on anymore. Boogie's face blurred out, until she slipped away into a peaceful darkness.

1994

Diana walked quickly through the hall of the hotel toward the elevator. She wanted to run, but a part of her hoped Barry would chase after her. When he never did, she felt her heart break all over again. When the elevator doors opened, she fell inside and leaned on the wall for support.

What started as a beautiful night had turned terrible. She'd held on to the hopes and dreams of one day Barry being hers, but that was all dead. She knew the kind of man Barry was, and that was a man who wouldn't walk out on his family. She would forever and always be something on the side, no matter how special he made her feel.

The elevator stopped finally, and she stood up straight and got off. She told herself that all she had to do was make it outside to her car. All she had to do was—a lurching feeling in her stomach made her stop in her tracks and double over a nearby trash can.

She threw up everything in her stomach, including the chocolate strawberries Barry had fed her. When she was done, she wiped her mouth with the back of her hand and stood upright. There were so many eyes on her, yet nobody came to check and see if she was okay. She had never felt so alone in her life.

Diana rushed through the tall doors of the building and didn't stop until she was in her BMW. Her hand rummaged through her purse in search of her car keys. When she found them, her hands were shaking so much she dropped them on the ground.

"Dammit!" she exclaimed and hit the steering wheel.

It was all just too much for her. She didn't even try to hold her tears back. Diana just let them fall. She let her head drop, and she sobbed so hard that her shoulders shook. She let everything out for a good five minutes before she sniffled and tried to stop crying.

Her fingers found their way in her purse again. That evening, she had planned on gifting Barry with the greatest gift a woman could give a man. It was the thing that could have made him hers had it not been for the baby growing inside of his wife. Diana wrapped her hands around what she was looking for and pulled it out. It was a pregnancy test. A positive pregnancy test.

She thought Barry was going to be so happy to know that she was having his baby. In her mind, she'd had it all planned out, but in the end, she didn't even want to tell him. After his news, Diana felt she would be a second thought. A burden. She placed her hand over her stomach and looked down at it.

"Don't worry. I'll figure it out. I always do."

Chapter 21

Boogie was still trying to wrap his head around what Diana had just told him. She and Barry had a baby? There were so many questions, but none of them could be answered unless he found her. Bentley and Gino came running back inside the restaurant just as Diana lost consciousness.

"Shit," Bentley said. "She's in bad shape, bruh."

"I need you to get them to the hospital, now. Gino, I need you to scrub all the security footage before the feds get here."

"Got it. Where you goin'?" Gino asked.

"To tie up one last loose end," Boogie said and left them to it.

He ran out of the building just in time to see Dina dragging Morgan to her Jeep down the street. He pushed his legs to go as fast as they could before they were gone and he couldn't get Morgan back.

Dina was strong for her age. Morgan was fighting, but she couldn't get away. However, she was slowing Dina down. Boogie reached them just as Dina was trying to force her in the driver's seat.

"Let her go, Mama. She ain't got nothing to do with this." Boogie pointed his gun at her face. "Don't make me shoot you!"

"Your bullet will probably meet my skull the same as mine meets hers," she sneered. "I saw how much Diana cares for her. She's my ticket."

"Just let her go."

"You can have her back after I sell my half of the businesses," she said and jubilantly patted her oversized purse. "I have everything I want now."

"I guess now is the best time to tell you that the papers in that folder are bullshit. I typed them up myself. I knew you would only look for a signature and not read anything else."

"You lie!"

"I'm not. Got you. Plus, I think I'd rather give part ownership of my businesses to my sister."

"You don't have a sister."

"I do. I guess you were right about Diana and my father having an affair. They had a baby girl."

"W–what? I fuckin' knew it! Who is she?" Dina exclaimed, enraged.

Boogie didn't say anything. His eyes fell on Morgan's, and in that moment, he noticed that they were identical to his. A realization fell over her, and her eyes widened.

"M–me?"

"Yes. You."

"No." Dina shook her head in disbelief. "No! I'm going to kill both of you." She took her eyes off Boogie to focus on Morgan. She cocked the gun back, and Morgan screamed. Boogie only had a split second to make a decision. In the end, he chose his father's legacy.

Bang!

"Uht!" Dina's face was frozen in shock as she choked on her air. She looked down and saw a bloody circle forming in the center of her chest. "Y–you shot me."

Those were her last words before she fell back onto her car and slid down. Her head rolled to one side when she hit the ground and took her last breath.

He never thought that he would be the one to take his mother's life, but in the end, he had no remorse about it. As he stood looking over her dead body, he felt nothing. Sirens could be heard in the distance, and Morgan tugged on his arm.

"Come on," she said. "I need to get to Diana."

Chapter 22

The distorted sound of voices invaded Diana's dream, and she tried to go back to focusing on the pretty garden in her mind, but the more she tried, the more she was pulled away from the colorful grassland. She groaned in agitation and felt a pain in her throat as she came back to consciousness. She was able to open her eyes completely, blinking feverishly at the bright light coming from the window.

She was in a bedroom, but not just any bedroom. It was one that had all of the things she loved in it. Plants hung from the ceiling, and the walls were painted blue and yellow, just like her room at the Big House.

"She's awake." A voice sounded on her right side.

She turned her head weakly to see who it belonged to and smiled when she saw the familiar face. Caesar smiled back at her.

"What happened?" she whispered.

"You gave me the scare of my life, that's what happened," he said with a concerned expression. "I expected you to come back in one piece, but when Marco brought you, you were barely alive."

"Marco?"

"Yeah, I called him." Another voice sounded, and Diana turned to see Boogie sitting on the edge of the bed.

"This motherfucka was tryna take you to the hospital." Diana heard Marco's voice. He was standing in the far corner. "And he's lucky Caesar called and told me everything that was goin' on, otherwise I would have tried to knock his head off. You still owe me for the warehouse you blew up, kid."

"And you'll get it. I'll earn all of your trust back. Especially yours, Caesar," Boogie said.

Diana looked from him to Caesar and wondered how that conversation had gone. Caesar nodded his head and turned back to Diana and gave her a knowing look.

"When Marco brought them all here, you would have thought they saw a ghost when they saw me. I guess technically, I was one to them," he explained. "I wanted the truth about my survival to stay under wraps for a little longer, but under the circumstances, I didn't really have a choice."

"When Marco brought . . . them all here?" Diana inquired, and Caesar smiled.

"I guess the Big House isn't an exclusive hideout anymore," Caesar said and pointed to the other side of her. "And I didn't think you had any secrets from me. Turns out I was wrong."

Diana slowly turned her head to the other side of the bedroom, where she was met by three faces: Bentley, Gino, and Morgan. Diana breathed a happy breath, and tears came to her eyes when she saw her daughter.

"Morgan," she whispered.

"Hi," Morgan said shyly.

She'd never been shy with Diana before, but then again, she also hadn't known she was her birth mother. Diana held her hand out, and Morgan approached the bed.

"There's so much that I need to explain to you," Diana said, clutching Morgan's fingers. "I know you must have so many questions."

"I do, but they can be asked another day," Morgan told her. "Right now you should rest."

"Okay, but I need to know, are you angry with me?"

"No," Morgan answered earnestly. "Whatever reason you had for giving me up, I'm sure it had something to do with protecting me."

The two of them stared lovingly at each other. Diana didn't know if it was because she was injured or if Morgan truly didn't harbor any bad feelings toward her. She'd played over and over how she would tell Morgan who she truly was, or if she would ever do it. Right there, staring up at her, Diana wanted to tell her that she'd never truly left her. That she'd been at every recital and that she was there when she graduated. It got to the point where she couldn't keep her distance anymore, which was why she had hired her on at the Sugar Trap. Her selfishness led her to bring Morgan back into the life she had tried to save her from.

"I'm sorry. I didn't mean to bring you into all of this," she said. Guilt riddled her as she lay in that bed, and Morgan read it over her face.

"Don't do that. It's not your fault. If I would have stayed in the van like you told me to, none of this would have happened. I always wondered where I got my hardheadedness from."

"Probably a fair amount from us both." Diana gave her a small smile and then let her hand go so she could turn back to Boogie. "What happened to your mother?"

"*Dina* is dead. I shot her," he answered solemnly.

"Oh, Boogie. I'm so sorry."

"Why? I'm not." Boogie shrugged. "She tried to take everything from me. Everything I was, and everything I loved. I sent her to hell where she belonged."

"Are you sure you're okay?"

"Nah, but I'll get there eventually."

"You know, when you were a boy, I—"

"I know," Boogie told her.

"And you know I still—"

"I know," he interrupted her again.

She let the tears fall freely from her eyes, and that was saying a lot, because Diana didn't let anyone see her cry. Morgan leaned down and kissed her forehead before making her way to the exit.

"I'm gonna go check on Tazz," she said. "Well, more so get on his nerves."

"You're makin' yourself at home with the family already I see." Boogie grinned at her, and she shrugged.

"I'll come with you. It's gettin' too sentimental in here for me." Gino hopped up, and Bentley followed behind him.

When they were gone, all that was left were the four family heads. Diana sat up, and Caesar fluffed some pillows behind her back.

"What happened with the Italians?" she asked Boogie.

"Exiled. I still run the territory, but that alliance was doomed from the start. Their loyalty will never be to me because it started in blood."

"Good."

"So, what's next for us?" Diana found herself inquiring out loud.

"Well, I think it's safe to say the pact is demolished," Caesar stated. "And I'm starting to be all right with that."

"What?" Marco asked, wide-eyed. "How will there be order between the families then?"

"We'll let the new blood decide that," Caesar answered and let his eyes fall on Boogie. "Just like we had to make our own way, let them."

"We've seen how well that's gone so far," Marco said.

"I think you forget how many mistakes were made when we were young, Marco. There are no lessons in perfection."

"Here you go with this old wise man's crap," Marco grumbled.

"You're such an angry old man." Diana chuckled. "You know what would look good on you?"

"What?"

"Retirement. I think that would look good on all of us."

"Retirement?" Marco made a face and looked to Caesar, who was nodding his head. "Wait. You can't agree with this. Are you saying that you're letting Nicky keep your spot as head of the borough?"

"That's exactly what I'm saying. Boogie needs people that can be on his level with him."

"Yeah, but that nigga probably hates me," Boogie chimed in sheepishly.

"He'll learn that you all are stronger together than separate."

"I'll think about it, but I'm not making any promises to step down," Marco said, crossing his arms.

"What about you, Diana? Who's gon' take your place?"

"I have someone in mind," Diana said fondly. "But until then, you will be in charge."

"Me?" Boogie asked incredulously.

"Yes, you. Just until Morgan is ready."

"If that's all out of the way, I think it's time to address the elephant in the room," Caesar stated. "Li. The Chinese aren't going to take kindly to us allowing Boogie back into the fold. They're going to strike back eventually."

BOOM! BOOM! BOOM! BOOM!

The sound of loud artillery caught all of them off guard, and it was followed by a loud bang. It came from outside of the house. Boogie and Caesar rushed to the window, while Marco pulled a Desert Eagle from his waist. Boogie and Caesar peered outside, and Diana heard Caesar curse under his breath.

She struggled out of the bed and rested her hand over the bandage on her stomach as she limped to the window. When she looked outside, she understood why Caesar had cursed. She looked at the gate and saw Malcom's body hanging out of the window of his guard post, dead. A swarm of black vehicles approached the house and came to a screeching stop. The car doors swung open, and out hopped more Chinese men than she could count. They were heavily armed and headed their way. Diana's heart pounded as she looked at Caesar.

"I guess eventually is today."

To be continued . . .